The River
Has No Camera

Anjali Chandran

The River Has No Camera

Anjali Chandran

Srishti
PUBLISHERS & DISTRIBUTORS

SRISHTI PUBLISHERS & DISTRIBUTORS
64-A, Adhchini
Sri Aurobindo Marg
New Delhi 110 017
First published by SRISHTI PUBLISHERS & DISTRIBUTORS in 2001
Copyright © Anjali Chandran

Rs. 195.00
ISBN 81-87075-26-0

Cover Design by Creative Concept
40/223 C R Park
New Delhi 110 019

Printed and bound in India by
Saurabh Print-O-Pack
A-16, Sector IV, Noida

For my father, on his seventieth birthday.

Acknowledgements

I'd like to thank my mother and sister, Julius Punnen, Sudeep Chowdhry, Ashutosh Raghuvanshi, Shobha Basavanaiah, Divi and Remi for the all encouragement. We had a great time with this book, didn't we?

Anjali

Contents

Part One

One

Thiruvathira Njaatuvela

I dragged the last piece of luggage out of the train and turned to look at the deserted Cheriathur station. I must have been the only person to whom Cheriathur had some significance on that day. It was the twenty-second of June, nineteen hundred and eighty five. I remember to this day, thirteen years later. Behind me, the train — it's whistle-stop over — trundled slowly out of the station. There was something unreal and dream-like about the moment. As if the train had deposited me in a magical land. Or perhaps atop a tree.

I think it was the rooster that made me feel that way. He stood on top of the wooden bench before me and looked at me quizzically, his head cocked to one side showing a three-quarter profile. Hanging on either side of his comb were gold earrings. Have you ever seen a rooster with gold earrings? I hadn't, and it amazed me. He was clearly a pampered rooster. Every now and then, he'd toss his glorious red comb and his earrings would sway about in the fading light, like little golden fireflies. His body was white as milk, each feather of his magnificent tail beautifully arranged, as if set with mousse. A truly handsome fellow.

I stood there staring at him partly because he amazed me but mainly because I was trying to collect my thoughts and decide what I must do next. My father had written to a distant relative asking him to come and receive me at Cheriathur. All I knew about this relative was that his name was Nandakumar and that he was related to my mother, from her grandfather's side of the family. Probably related by some common DNA. But a stranger nevertheless. No face. No form. Just a name. Where was he, anyway? I kept watch, expecting any moment to see someone walk in and apologize profusely. But nobody came.

It was getting dark, and there was a distinct smell of rain in the air. I looked up at the sky. Clouds hung low over the station and grew darker even as I stood gazing at them. A gust of wind lifted the leaves of a young banana tree on the other side of a broken down fence behind the platform, making the tree look like a nubile young thing caught in an embarrassing moment with her skirt ballooning in the wind. Yes, this was definitely rain — all the signs pointed to it. I moved to the covered section of the platform, observing the darkening forms of trees loom like giant beanstalks over the short platform. The walls of the stationmaster's cabin and the rooster were the only things glowing

4

white in that odd, ambiguous light.

I smelled wood smoke, and promptly conjured in my imagination the figure of a woman cooking for her family. It made my eyes brim with unwitting tears. Sentimental images — like that of a family sitting down to a meal together — always do this to me. Sentimental fool that I am. The kind of person who laughs till she cries.

But it wasn't merely that. There was one other thing. The image of that family — never mind that it was only an image (and, for all you know, the smell may have been that of burning garbage) — made me lonelier still. The sense of loneliness is a constant, often hidden in secret recesses. But this chance reminder, evoked by the aroma of wood smoke, revived it. Revived the sense that I always have of standing outside, alone, all by myself. Always the watcher, never the watched. Ever the *watcher*, not the *watchee*.

~

A big raindrop fell on the platform, followed by another. Within seconds, it began raining as if it had been raining forever and would never stop. It was the month of *Mithunam*. *Mithunam maasam, thiruvathira njaatuvela* — the *njaatuvela* of the rain. Every *nakshatra* — or star — has a *njaatuvela* that lasts fifteen days, and the *njaatuvela* of the star *Thiruvathira* is in the month of *Mithunam*. According to the Malayalam calendar, *Edavam, Mithunam* and *Karkitakam* are the months of rain, and the *mithunam maasam thiruvaatira njaatuvela* heralds the monsoon in Kerala — a monsoon that show no signs of letting up until the end of *Karkitakam* in early August.

The rain drummed on the asbestos roof of the platform shutting out all other sounds and adding a new aspect to my predicament. I wiped my palms on the side of my *kurta* and sat down. I was nervous and my palms were moist with sweat. My eyes were burning. I closed them, pressing my lids tightly together until I could see fluorescent graffiti moving in slow motion on a black screen. This journey had been — and still was — a difficult one. I had left Bombay scarred, confused and estranged from myself.

By the time I actually left Bombay, I had begun to hate it. It was full of memories, but none pleasant or happy. They were the sort of memories that one is always trying to forget. Ghosts and demons leapt out of corners to haunt and to taunt me, and I was relieved to leave finally. But that evening, sitting all by myself at a strange railway station and listening to the deafening torrent of rain, I began to miss Bombay, the city of my childhood. My city! I missed the crowds. I missed my life there. My identity, my family, my friends — the bonds that give a person a sense of security.

I had left all that and come here to start a new life. I had taken a bold step into the unknown, into an uncharted alien territory. People might think it was a feisty thing to have done, except that right then I wasn't feeling particularly feisty. Quite the opposite. I felt more like a small child in a new school. New sights. New sounds. New smells. How important it is for children to have familiar smells around them, for them to sleep, to eat, to *be*. It's only we adults who need to reassure ourselves that we're never nervous or scared, and that everything's okay and in control.

I have a confession to make, though. I'm not going to pretend any of these things. I've been telling you right from the start that I was a mess, a twitching wreck. Why I was so is a long story that will gradually unfold as the doors within me slowly open.

~

*S*itting there waiting for Mr. Nandakumar, I imagined all kinds of reasons as to why he hadn't come. His wife was delivering a baby. His son had a test at school. Today might be the *Grihapravesham* for his new house. I imagined him to be a family man. Content. Immersed in family and family affairs — like everyone but me. These thoughts left me more depressed. I felt alienated and unloved and, somehow, unworthy, even filthy. Filthy, like an unflushed toilet. But I didn't want to feel that way. I was always doing this to myself. Inviting thoughts that left me feeling lousy, and then trying to struggle against the lousy feeling. Not coming to terms with them. Scared to look them in the eye. Always running away. I could just as easily have put his absence down to the rain — perhaps he didn't have a vehicle. But no, I didn't do that. I thought instinctively of all the possibilities that I knew would make me depressed. I had become my own worst enemy.

It's easy for me to say all this now. But at that time I couldn't be objective the way I am now. I couldn't stand aside and watch me the way I'd sit in a theatre and watch a movie. At that time, *I* was the movie.

Not that I'm wonderfully objective about my life today. I'm still wondering which way it went.

~

Where was this Nandakumar? I sat there, getting more and more morose by the minute. I could feel the depression ferment in my stomach like undigested *biryani*. It was a horrible, ugly feeling; a churning, an emotional retching. I hated it and tried desperately to push it — that Thing -- out of my mind. But how does one get rid of the Thing that is a dead weight. Debris. A result of mangled memories and feelings. I wanted to sweep it away with a single brush of my hand. But how? At that time I didn't have the answers I have today; just as today, I don't have the answer I might have tomorrow. I wanted to bottle the Thing up and hide it away in some inaccessible dungeon deep inside my mind. Maybe when enough time had gone by — a thousand years — the Thing in the bottle would be reduced to nothing. Dust and fluff. All I'd need to do then would be to wash the bottle and put it to dry in the sun. Simple — like the instructions behind a bottle of shampoo! *Bottle, wait a thousand years, rinse. Don't repeat.*

It was beginning to seem Mr. Nandakumar wasn't going to arrive. I tried to concentrate on what I should do next. Maybe I

8

should find Alanghat, my *tharavaat* — ancestral house. Alanghat was the reason for my leaving Bombay. Alanghat was the place I was going to make my home from now on. The place I had always known but had never seen. The place where my family had lived for one hundred and thirty five years of recorded history.

Legend has it that one of my ancestors, Alanghat Shankunni Nair, had been given 25,000 acres of land as *dhanapramanam*, a gift, by the Raja of Kollengode for having fought a heroic battle against the troops of Hyder Ali. When told by the king to ask for anything he wanted, Shankunni Nair modestly asked for all the land that could be seen from Ayappan Para, the highest hill in Kunnathur. One could see all of 25,000 acres from there, and the Raja gave it without batting an eyelid. Thus it was that Alanghat Shankunni Nair became the biggest landlord — *jenmie* — in the district. But Alanghat was in shambles now, just as I was. I was here to resurrect it and in the process, rise like the phoenix.

~

*I*t was getting very late and the rain had eased to a heavy drizzle. I would have to get up and do something now. But what? I opened my eyes and found a man standing in front of me, with his *mundu* folded at half-mast, displaying a pair of scrawny legs that somehow reminded me of boiled eggs. A big black umbrella hung from his collar down his back and he had a rolled-up newspaper in his hand. His mouth hung open on that gnome-like face. Another half-forgotten memory of a fairy-tale stirred awake. *Binkity, the Naughty Gnome*. But why was he staring at me? I had a sudden vision of myself, as he must see me. Sitting all by myself, with my eyes closed, on the wooden bench of a tiny whistle-stop station, deep in the heart of Kerala. Cheriathur was the sort of place people knew only because they passed the station on their way to other places and read the yellow and black signpost. Nobody ever actually chose to get off here. So where had I come from? Why wasn't I going anywhere? Yes, it was odd. Decidedly odd. No wonder he was gaping. I bestowed on him the right to gape.

It so turned out that he was the stationmaster and he recieved his second surprise in less than five minutes when I told him I wanted to go to Alanghat. It must have been my poor Malayalam because I should have actually said I wanted to go to Kunnathur, the place where Alanghat was located. But what I said didn't sound quite right. I was about to rephrase the sentence when I noticed his reaction. Behind his black-framed spectacles his round eyes popped out as he stood gaping, his mouth open even wider than before. I didn't think I had said anything to warrant such a theatrical response and it bewildered me. In any case, I hadn't even told him where the blessed house was! Imagine standing at Victoria Terminus Station in Bombay, telling someone that you want to go to "Sunshine ". He'll think you're crazy.

This man, however, didn't think I was crazy. I seemed to have made perfect sense to him and that baffled me. Feeling my way cautiously, I asked him if he knew the place and he muttered that he most certainly did. It struck me that perhaps he doubled as the postmaster and that's how he knew. I couldn't ask him outright, so I asked him if he knew all the houses in Kunnathur. That exasperated him. He sat down with a whoosh, whisking his umbrella from behind him in the nick of time. It was the kind with a little frill at the beginning of a long pointed end. 'Alanghat isn't just any house', he said, shaking his left hand with each finger outstretched and rolling his eyes. He had a flat unmusical voice, like the horn of a truck. And also a slight nasal sound to it as if his spectacles pressed down too hard on his nose. It made me itch to lift them up by the bridge. He stared at me grimly for a second and then, turning his hand into a fist with the little finger sticking out, he asked me why I wanted to go there.

I told him I was going to live there from now on and that's how the poor man got his third shock in five minutes. Why that should shock him, I couldn't for the life of me fathom. We stared at each other, me completely foxed and him completely shocked; him sitting and me standing. Suddenly inspired, I said, 'I am Keshavan Nair's great-granddaughter.'

This time it was my turn to be shocked. I had introduced myself only so that my appearance should cease to mystify him. I belonged to that house, for God's sake! So why shouldn't I want to stay there? But no, the man had to react to everything I said by rolling his eyes, gasping or gaping. What I hadn't realised was that all this was mere B-grade, amateur stuff compared to what he was about to come up with now. He rocketed upwards with an '*Ende*

11

Bhagwati!' -- 'My Goddess' — a literal, unpoetic sort of translation but the best I can offer at the moment — letting down the half-mast and landing twenty feet away from me, quivering and silent.

Flabbergasted, I stared at him for a good three seconds before the coin dropped. He knew the story! All of Cheriathur and the other *urs*' nearby must know! You see, Alanghat — illustrious, aristocratic Alanghat — has had to live with a rather sordid past. It had been the eye of a storm for years. Strange tales had been spun around it by the local people. Tales that were based nine-tenths on temple gossip, and one-tenth on facts. I don't think any of these people had ever expected to see another person from the Alanghat House again. Especially not after all these years — a quarter of a century. No wonder this funny fellow, Binkity, was shell-shocked.

~

I should have expected this, really. What a fool I was to think that I could come here and bury myself. *Here*, of all places! Instead, I was going to occupy the centre stage. The hot white spotlight. It had never occurred to me that Alanghat could be sort of in the centre of things in Kunnathur. It should have but it didn't. And so I had never considered the effect my sudden arrival might have on the people there. In any case, as a rule, what other people thought figured only very hazily in my scheme of things. If it figured at all. So I was unprepared for all the attention I was about to receive.

I stood there staring at Binkity as all this sank in. All at once I felt defeated. I was reaching the end of my tether. Had already reached it. I felt my shoulders droop and the sides of my mouth began to quiver. I was tired, dirty, hungry and close to tears. I tried to cover it up. Pretend everything was fine. I could not let him know I was all crummy inside. I used to be like that. I could not let anybody know what I really felt about anything. I had to be flippant or nonchalant. The more I hurt, the more blasé I became. It was a sort of ego thing, you know. Always wear the mask of indifference. Like a perfectly made-up face. No visible scars. No pimples. No wrinkles. Nothing to reveal. That way your pride is always intact. Sometime later, when you're completely lost and confused, you can always unlearn the last twenty years and start again. At leisure, in the privacy of your own hell.

You'll have to forgive me for digressing like this. But you'll have to put up with it. It's important for me that I tell you all this.

I suddenly remembered that my father had given me Mr. Nandakumar's address on a piece of paper. He had written down the telephone number too. I found the paper and asked the stationmaster if I could make a call. He took me into his tiny cabin and pushed the ancient black phone towards me. I dialed the two-digit number. The dial turned slowly, with a loud, creaking sound. When I dialed zero, it took forever to turn. After three or four attempts, I concluded there was something wrong with either the number or the line. I slowly turned to Binkity and once again asked him where Alanghat was. This time he answered me in plain words, without any comic relief; adding that, as far as he knew, the place had been locked up for twenty five years. Ever since ... .

I remained silent, offering no cue to his narrative.

'At this time of the night,' he continued, diplomatically leaving his earlier sentence incomplete, 'Is it safe to go there?' He was right. 'Any hotels?' He made a gesture with his fingers and thumb signifying that there was nothing worthwhile. Silently, he lifted one of my bags. 'My grandmother worked as a cook at Alanghat many years ago, and so did her mother,' he said.

'You can stay with me if you wish. Tomorrow we can go to Alanghat.'

He sounded humble and that irritated me. I preferred the pompous stationmaster. And why was he being humble? Because I had a family that had tricked, fought and killed each other nearly to extinction while his hadn't? I considered my options. I could land up at Nandakumar's house. But that would amount to the same thing as staying at Binkity's. He was as much a stranger to me as this man. Also, it seemed significant to me that for some reason he hadn't come to receive me at the station. It looked like I didn't have too many options. So I thanked him and followed him out of the station.

He took me to his house by a short-cut behind the station. A muddy, nondescript sort of lane. Or maybe that was the right way — I don't know. I remember that lane so well because I thought it would go on forever and ever. My bags were that heavy.

I wondered about his readiness to accept me for what I said I

14

was. I was from Bombay, the Big City — the Big C. Where no one trusts anyone. Why was he being so nice to me — inviting me to his house and all that? And why was I following him so obediently? I knew the answer to that. I was sure that he was a good man and that he meant what he said. In fact, I didn't doubt him at all. It must have been his simplicity and lack of guile. Perhaps rustic India was like this. Hospitable to a fault. The true Indian tradition. *Yeh Purab hai Purab Wale* … . Manoj Kumar. Or is it Raj Kapoor?

None of the above. The answer, as it turned out, was the former eminence of Alanghat. Though it had its share of tyrannical and oppressive *zamindars*, Alanghat had by and large treated tenants fairly well. And people, especially people in small places, don't forget. In its days of greatness, Alanghat had kept an open kitchen and everybody was welcome to have a meal, no matter what the time. Things like that count, you know.

My family — especially the women, like my great-grandmother, Rugmani Devi Amma — had been gracious and hospitable. Always smiling. Though the system was wholly feudal, Alanghat had not been a cruel family. Useless, yes. Cruel, no. There's a word for people like them in Malayalam. *Kollaraathather.* Like many other affluent Nair families around, the cause of our downfall too had been wine and women. All the Alanghat men had been playboys — handsome, rich and good-for-nothing.

The other reason was my great-grandfather, Keshavan Nair, Rugmani Devi's husband. He is something of a legend in these parts though not originally from Alanghat. I don't know for sure

15

but I think he was from *Vattavompaday*, another Nair *tharavaat*. I don't know more than that so please don't bother asking. Anyway, this bit is not relevant to my story. Apparently, he was scrupulously fair in all his dealings — stern and unapproachable. They say he used to roll his eyes and roar when angry. A Kathakali dancer, his only hobby was dancing. And since Keshavan Nair was the only capable man Alanghat had at that time, they clung unconditionally to him. His word was law in Alanghat, and in all of Kunnathur.

Keshavan Nair was also something of a reformer and an activist. He started the first girl's school in Kunnathur, and for many years this school — the Rugmani Devi English Medium School for Girls, Kunnathur — was the only school for girls for miles around. That was way back in the thirties. The good thing about the school was that it was free for poor children. Every *Visu*, the Malayali New Year, Rugmani Devi stood in the porch of Alanghat distributing a *visukayneetam* of a set of notebooks, a slate, two pencils, two skirts, two blouses and a lice comb to all the children who were studying there on scholarship.

Because of Keshavan Nair's "odd" ideas, Rugmani Devi could speak, read and write fluent English, she could understand Hindi and had authored a Malayalam cookbook, which was published by Keshavan Nair. My mother has a copy gifted to her by Rugmani Devi herself. The first page has the words:

My dearest Ammu,
If winter comes, can spring be far behind?

16

For you on your sixteenth birthday.
From Ammuma, with all my love.
17th April, 1947

Whenever I read the words, *with all my love*, my eyes fill up. Lucky Ammu, to have received love like that. I would have given anything to be as fortunate. There was an acute need in me to be loved at that time,.

The handwriting is rounded and child-like, the ink has now faded and the paper is brown with age. Rugmani Devi died that same year. The year Ammu, my mother, turned sixteen. So she never found just how long that winter actually was and what a vicious sting it carried in its tail.

Keshavan Nair had also started the first veterinary hospital in that area. It was called the Rugmani Devi Veterinary Hospital, Kunnathur. He brought a vet all the way from Coimbatore and paid him eighty rupees a month — a king's ransom in those days.

Nobody doubted the fact that Alanghat flourished solely because of Keshavan Nair. Not even his brothers-in law. So they treated him with a good deal of caution. But unfortunately, they were not accountable to him. Or to anyone else. That's the funny thing about the matrilineal system of the Nair*s*. Though the property belonged to women, their brothers had all the power and ran the estate. That was why it was important to have capable men. Neither of Rugmani Devi Amma's brothers was interested in nurturing the enormous family wealth. They were more interested in spending it recklessly rather than in adding to it. Thus, it was left to Keshavan Nair, who was not even from Alanghat, to take care of the estate. But he was the last of his kind, like Aurangzeb. After him, there was nothing but decay — eminently forgettable people. And that is why I chose to introduce myself as his great-granddaughter.

~

*B*ack to Binkity. By way of introduction, he merely told his wife that I was of Alanghat House and that I had come to live in Kunnathur. I was told nothing and was left to put two and two together and assume that the lady in front of me was Mrs. Binkity. Her reaction to the word Alanghat was as noticeable as her husband's and her manner towards me became ingratiating, almost servile. It reminds me now of those hyenas in *The Lion King*. That Whoopi Goldberg thing, you know.

She had a quarrelsome look about her. Binkity's wife, not Whoopi. I think it was her nose — it was pinched at the tip, not large and generous. My heart sank the moment I set eyes on her. I knew instantly that she'd hold court at the temple the following evening. The temple is the hub of all social activity in places like Kunnathur. The vortex. And, for once, she, Binkity's wife, would be the one with the news. All the Thangamanis and Parukuttys of Cheriathur would have to shut up and listen. And how they would listen! By morning, the day after — I calculated — the whole district would know that someone from the infamous house was back. Not just anyone but a young, single woman.

I ate very little and in silence — Binkity's wife wasn't much of a cook. I watched as she cleared the table and wiped the bright blue sheet of plastic that covered it. *You've never had an orgasm, have you?* The thought had formed and whizzed through my mind before I could slap it away. I was getting tired of slapping thoughts away but these were dangerous waters. No, I couldn't handle complex things like orgasms in the state of mind I was in, even if they were the ones Binkity's wife had never had. They brought back memories. My body seemed to have a memory of its own, and it stubbornly remembered, in glorious detail, the things my mind was trying so desperately to forget.

How long was I to go on suppressing every thought — every memory — pushing it away, slapping it down! I knew that one day I would have to sit down and open my little *potli* of debris and do some spring cleaning ... one distant day — not now. Now was too immediate, and it called for too much bravery.

I had no control over my thoughts. The slightest thing could send me spiraling into the deepest depression. I was terrified of them and they made me sick with fear and anxiety. The only thing I could do was to block them, slap them down before they popped out of their holes. So I repeated 'Later, not now' to myself like a litany. I didn't stop to consider whether *later* would make it any easier. Or whether *later* would render the whole exercise unnecessary. I just didn't want to it to be NOW. The *not now* changed from a hysterical command to a desperate plea. But no matter how hard I begged, I couldn't arrest the distress that whirled into my mind like a sudden sandstorm. I suddenly pushed my chair back and got up.

The metallic noise of the chair scraping against the floor grated on my taut nerves. The familiar feeling of restlessness had returned and I felt sick in my stomach. I stood in the centre of the tiny room, holding my breath, my jaws clenched — trying desperately to force it out. It was beginning to swamp me and I hated it. I knew that if I didn't fight it, it would drown me completely. I *had* to fight. I *had* to press it down till it stopped suffocating me.

I don't know how long I stood shadow boxing. Perhaps a minute. When I looked up, Binkity was standing by the door holding out a towel and saying something. Good idea! I reached out and grabbed the towel as if it were a life jacket. I would take a bath.

The bathroom had an old warped door which had once, way back in its distant youth, been painted blue. The bottom of the door had been eaten away by water. There was a clothesline hanging right across, on which hung so many clothes that I was scared to add my clothes to it. Suppose the whole thing collapsed? I hung my clothes on the top of the door, where there was a gap between the tiled roof and the frame of the door. A naked bulb hung by a wire from the beams above, swinging slightly in the breeze that blew through the room. The whole room had a dingy look about it; a massive toad in one corner making an immodest contribution to the almost creepy ambience.

But there was a positive side. The room had an old copper

drum with handles on either side, and someone had filled them with hot water. The water felt pleasantly warm and I thoroughly enjoyed the first mug. The journey from Bombay had been a long one and I had had to change trains once to reach Cheriathur. It had been three days since I had last bathed properly. I washed my hair — rough with grime — and scrubbed every inch of my body until I tingled all over. Gradually, I felt the tension ebb.

That was a good bath. It really was. The floor of the bathroom was made of granite and I scrubbed my heels on the slab until they hurt. For days after that I had to walk on tiptoe, but at that moment it had seemed the most fitting thing to do. By the time I toweled myself dry I was myself again.

Back inside the house (the bathroom was outside in the back courtyard), I found Binkity waiting for me in the centre room. I asked him if I could get a taxi to take me to Kunnathur tomorrow morning. He said he could arrange that. Apparently, his neighbor's son owned a private taxi. That fixed, I went into my room to dry my hair and go to bed. Hopefully, to sleep.

Two

But there was no sleep. I lay with my eyes shut all night and woke up the next morning, tired with the effort. There was a time — many lives ago — before everything — a time when I could sleep curled like a puppy. More recently, things had changed. Night after night I'd lie wide-awake, with my eyes shut tight, waiting for the day to dawn.

~

I arose at the first sign of life. The rain had lashed and howled all night long and had now subsided into a tired drizzle. Cows lowed in the distance and once again I smelled the familiar smell of burning wood. I heard the temple playing the *Vishnu Sahasranamam* on the tannoy; M.S. Subbulakshmi's voice wafted across the paddy fields — *Shuklambaradaram Vishnum Shashivarnam Chaturbhujam* ... .

After another trip to the dingy bathroom, I joined Binkity's wife in the kitchen. I tried to convince her to let me help but she wouldn't hear of it. After a while I gave up and took my tumbler of coffee out into the enclosed verandah in the front of the house. I sat there looking through a black, red and white grill into a small courtyard. The grill, I couldn't help noticing, was adorned with a design of hand-painted red fish swimming between black lotuses. On one side of the gate was a large hibiscus bush, bursting with flowers. The other side had *pavizhamalli* that had flowered in the night, and now carpeted the earth with small coral-stalked flowers. Wherever I looked, there were different colours. The sky was a watery blue, the distant hills were misty purple, and the neighbouring houses were sort of Robin-Liquid-Blue white. The earth was dark rust, wet with rain. Fields of emerald filled all the gaps so not an inch of the canvas was bare.

I sat there holding the tumbler at the rim with both my hands, blowing loudly at the hot coffee to cool it, in between equally loud slurps. It wasn't something I would have done in Bombay. But here, it somehow didn't seem gross. I put down the empty tumbler and watched it rock on its unsteady base.

Why are they called tumblers? I mean, why *tumblers*? Was it because they tumbled and fell? But couldn't everything tumble and fall? Even Jill tumbled and fell. I am not too satisfied with that word. I think they ought to change it. Whoever decides these things should hold a meeting and change the name. It reminded me of the confusion I'd had for years with the word 'glass'. My mother would always say that *nimbu pani* should be served in *glass* glasses and not in *metal* glasses. Steel glasses were not to be used for serving guests. We had Yera glasses at the time — the squat, broad-rimmed ones, not the fashionable long narrow-rimmed ones. The long ones were for rich business people. The Sindhis.

I was toying with the idea of fetching another tumbler of coffee when I saw the stationmaster enter the courtyard with another, younger man; a taxi driver named Hari. A tall lean man with a stainless steel wristwatch that was much too big for him. He had a way of shaking it back almost every three seconds. He did that twelve times, during the time it took me to ask the stationmaster to accompany me to Alanghat. I had counted.

Hari's car was a white Ambassador. It had two yellow lines and one white line with a red dot in the centre painted on its windscreen. The lines and the dot denoted sandalwood paste, *vibhuti* and *kum kum*. I had never seen a more strangely decorated car in my life! It was a veritable mobile temple. A psychedelic Balaji graced the dashboard and blinked green and red when the engine started, giving the whole car an odd strobe-light effect. A plastic jasmine garland tasseled the windscreen from one end to the other, and a bunch of *agarbattis* burnt at the lotus feet of Balaji. The car had little brown curtains in the windows that refused to let in any light. The minute he got into the front seat and saw Balaji, Binkity touched the centre of his forehead and a point on his chest and devoutly gasped 'Krishna!'

We sat in silence throughout the drive. I couldn't look out of the window because of the curtains so I stared straight ahead, with half an eye on Binkity's right temple which reflected the red and green lights from Balaji's disco-altar. After a stony silence of about fifteen minutes, Hari decided to play some music, following which Binkity's temple throbbed green and red, in rhythm to *Paga ghungaroo baandh Mira naachi thi - naachi thi - naachi thi.* Amitabh Bachchan had reached Cheriathur too.

~

*I*t was a forty-minute drive from Cheriathur to Kunnathur. The land on either side of the road was draped in varying shades of green. In the distance were dense groves of coconut trees, their fronds thick and luxuriant. Small houses nestled in the deep shade of the groves, smoke rising from their chimneys, their thatched roofs hanging so low that they almost touched the ground. As we drove past, I caught a glimpse of a woman in a black blouse and a checked *mundu*, holding a *patta-chool* — a broom made from the dried veins of the coconut leaf — and scratching her head.

Huge hibiscus bushes of an ordinary variety — like the bush in Binkity's house — grew in the courtyards of homes. The bright red flowers seemed garish in the elegant green landscape, but their sensuous beauty merged so harmoniously with the rest of the landscape that it seemed there could be nothing more beautiful in this world. The place looked peaceful and serene, a balm to my jangled nerves.

After driving straight down the main road for some time, we reached an intersection. A concrete signpost displayed an arrow pointing left for Kunnathur, and one pointing heavenwards for Edavannur. We obediently turned left and within minutes, we were driving through what seemed to be the commercial quarter of Kunnathur.

This comprised six shops clustered around a small flagpole and a bus stop. Buntings from the last year's Independence Day celebration trailed messily from the flagpole. There was a grocery shop, popularly known to everyone (as I learnt later) as *Nandu inte kada*, Nandu's shop. There was a cloth shop — K.G. Textorium, a tailor, a *chai* shop, a butcher and a stainless steel shop — Kunnathur Stainless Steel Mart. The walls of the shops, the base of the flagpole and the culvert nearby were plastered with ragged cinema posters. Men in pink shirts and white *mundus* sat idly, shaking their legs, talking and spitting.

Ignoring their curious stares we drove past into an enclave of private houses. Here, the houses had high walls around them and small gates, with the names of the houses welded to the gates: *Lakshmi Nivas, Devi Vilas, Padmalaya, Kavesseri, Ambalalaya.*

We drove right through Kunnathur to the other side, and then began to climb a steep narrow road cut into a hillside. At the point where we turned, there was a sign nailed to a young *neem* tree: *Piles and Fistula Clinic, Manuthy. Dr. Shaikh-Mahaboob.* Piles and fistulas, indeed! What a wonderfully unique view Dr. Shaikh-Mahaboob must have of the world! Maybe it had been his mother's dying wish — 'MBBS *pass aaii* — after you pass your MBBS — you must open a Piles and Fistula Clinic in Manuthy.'

~

*T*he precipice of the small hill we were climbing was densely covered with all kinds of trees. I could spot jackfruit, mango and breadfruit. We crested the hill and stopped in front of a massive but otherwise unassuming gate, fitted into a high crumbling wall made of laterite. It was protected by a tiled monkey-top roof. The gate was barred and bolted with huge locks and had a smaller door fitted into it.

~

I had never seen Alanghat before, not even as a child. This was my first sight of the place. I got out of the car and searched for the keys. I have this thing about keys. Whenever I have to unlock something, I work myself up into a state. First, I worry about whether I have the right keys. Then I fumble through every pocket in my bag. Next, I wonder anxiously if I've dropped them somewhere. By this time, my companions are exasperated and start rattling the lock vigorously. As if that could help me find the key! And finally, when I find the bunch of keys, I drop it twice before the hunt for the right key begins. But I also forget which side of the bunch I started with, and try the same three keys in the lock seven times. By the time I manage to unlock the door, I am exhausted!

~

*H*ere too, we went through the entire sequence. Step by step. I had no time to think about the enormity of the occasion because I was a little too preoccupied with a huge bunch of the oddest-looking keys I had ever held in my hand. To be honest with you, I was apprehensive about this ceremonial unlocking since the time my mother gave me the keys.

It was only after I had fumbled and sweated and finally triumphed, that things began to fall in place. I realized that the massive door I had thought to be the entrance to the house was not that at all. It was, in fact, a sort of gatehouse, no more. There were rooms on either side, and a path led into a huge ground. I hadn't expected so much space on the other side of the wall. There must have been at least two cricket fields of land walled in. Half the hill.

~

*I*n front of me was an old and immense mango tree. A circular brick platform – now covered with ferns and moss, and even mushrooms – had been built around it. Branches grew along the ground, shaped like inviting hammocks. Alanghat looked like a verdant paradise that hadn't been disturbed for centuries. Long steps and low walls made of laterite bricks criss-crossed the place; so old and mossy that they looked natural and unplanned.

To the left of the tree was a hopeless ruin. My heart sank when I saw it, for it was beyond repair. Its roof had caved in, as if trampled by a clumsy giant. The white walls were broken and orange rubble lay scattered everywhere. The profusion of weeds growing on what had once been the floor of the building only reconfirmed that the place had remained untouched for a long time. There were no windows and no doors. Only holes to indicate that these had once been there. A young banyan tree growing out of a crack in the only intact wall completed the desolate picture. Behind this decrepit structure, barely visible, was another, much bigger building.

My heart fluttered back to its post, quickening its tempo until it sounded like a roll of thunder in my ears. I took a few steps to the left and stood staring at what lay in front of me.

~

*A*langhat looked back at me, straight in the eye. Neither proud nor servile, unpretentious and uninhibited, entirely comfortable with herself. Her simple, graceful proportions were haunting and beautiful — so beautiful that even the clouds seemed obliged to arrange themselves picturesquely overhead. I didn't have a camera and I didn't need one. I will remember that moment to my dying day.

She was huge and her tiled roof, with its peaks and valleys, reminded me of brown hills. The tiles sloped down, low over her walls, ending in a small lacy frill. The windows had tiled awnings with monkey-tops, as did the huge verandah on the first floor, right above the front porch. The ground floor had a long verandah running round the house, it's roof held up by big carved pillars of solid teak.

I walked across the overgrown courtyard, covered thick with dead mango leaves, to the front porch. The first sound I heard as I stepped in, was that of pigeons muttering comfortably to themselves on the roof.

Alanghat was almost entirely made of teak. There were three steps leading to the porch which was held up by four gigantic wooden pillars. The pillars were thick — almost obese — around the centre but tapered into a lotus-like shape. From the porch, we entered a long wide verandah that had carved teak benches running across its entire length. The front doors were massive, intricately carved and fitted with brass rings. Three iron bars ran across these, each carrying a heavy brass lock. My hands shook a little as I fumbled again with the keys. Finally, after what seemed like three hours, we had the front door open and were at last inside the house.

My thoughts were confused and chaotic. I felt drawn as if by some powerful magnet to the very core, the spirit of the place. The only other time I had felt this way was when I had first seen the *Shiva Kshetram* — the Shiva temple — at Chidambaram. I stood in the wide corridor and stared at the square space in the middle of the house, which opened to the sky. The roof converged over it in a V-shape and hundreds, or at least what seemed like hundreds, of wooden pillars — smaller versions of the ones outside — surrounded it. Rows of thick teak doors fitted into carved frames, and decorated with brass, opened into wide corridors that encased open space.

I turned around and saw the walls on either side of the front door lined with old family photographs. On both sides of the door were two raised platforms that supported rows of teakwood pillars. (Perhaps this was where Keshavan Nair did his Kathakali!) I climbed one of these to take a closer look at my forefathers – and *foremothers*, if there is such a word. The photographs were coated with dust and fungus, but for the eyes. The eyes, it seemed, had been left clear on purpose; so that they could follow me around. All those ancestral eyes. My spine tingled, and I felt the goose bumps on my arms.

Some were intriguing. A young man in a shirt, *mundu* and tennis shoes, stepping into a vintage motor car; a family portrait of a man, a woman and a young girl — the woman was wearing what looked like an off-white brocade silk sari, and her hair stuck to her head in rivulets that flowed down her temples; an arrogant looking man leaning back in a buggy driven by two horses, its driver sitting high up all by himself, holding a whip. I walked along till I reached a group photograph of all the residents of Alanghat, taken in front of the house in the year — I peered through the dust to decipher the date scrawled in one corner — 1928. There were fifteen rows of people with the family members seated in front, and the dogs at their feet. There was also an old and faded photograph of an elephant. Now I knew why Alanghat had needed such a massive gate. It had to accomodate a tusker.

The corridors were lined with huge paintings of men and women; the men attempting to look Byronic, but the women with a style of their own. Kohl-eyed and bejeweled. Regal. One of them was Keshavan Nair and another Rugmani Devi. I had no idea which. I recognised my mother though. A young, gauche girl of fourteen or fifteen — so different from the person I called my mother. I wondered what had happened to this girl in the photograph. Had she slipped away into some cave? Like Puff the Magic Dragon.How would it be if I were to meet the two-year-old that I once was, and the five-year-old that I once was, and the fourteen-year-old and the twenty-year-old. Would the five of us have anything to say to each other? Would we recognise each other? Or would we just walk past each other like strangers?

Walking around the house, I could almost hear voices, the sound of children playing, of lunch being cooked, of life being lived. There was an *aat-katal* in one of the rooms. It's heavy rosewood plank hung from the beams on four brass chains. The chains had elephants and peacocks worked into the loops. It was hard to

33

imagine that no one had sat on it for a quarter of a century. I almost saw my great-grandfather striding in and sitting down on it. A*lmost*!

The place was covered with dust and cobwebs and there was a gaping hole in the roof through which rain-water had poured in, wetting the thick layer of dust on the floor and making it difficult to walk on. The house was wrapped in a silence enhanced by the sound of rainwater that was still dripping from the roof. It was a sad sort of silence. A *mounam*.

Binkity activated his flat *Horn Please OK* voice and broke the spell with a loud snort. It sounded like a fart and seemed to echo in the empty house. Startled, I turned towards him. He too had been looking around and was now ready to give his verdict. It turned out to be no different from mine. Alanghat would need months of renovation and repair. And I would need an army of people to help me.

One of the rooms on the ground-floor had been converted into a makeshift kitchen, probably by my grandmother. She had lived here alone for some time. An empty Amul milk-powder can still sat on the bare shelf nailed to the wall. Some used matchsticks and crumpled newspaper lay on a small collapsible table. In the corner of the room there were two big Marie biscuit canisters, their rusty lids jammed tight. The real kitchen was outside the house. Like a sort of outhouse. Attached to it was what I suppose can be called a dining room. A long wide hall with windows on one side. There was a big spacious verandah in front, which, I presumed, was meant for the additional guests. I wondered how many people Alanghat must have fed on an average day. I imagined rows of banana leaves, and even began counting them. One hundred and twenty. A hundred and twenty people a day! For one meal!

Very different from that dingy, makeshift kitchen on the ground floor, with its Amul milk-powder can and Marie biscuit canisters. I decided immediately to use the big kitchen and not that dingy room. Even if it was only to make coffee. Not practical, I know. But who ever said that one must be practical? Anyone who goes around telling people that, does untold harm. Take it from me. Life is not about being practical. I don't know exactly what it is about, but it is definitely not about being practical.

~

*T*he kitchen had six stoves fitted into a soot-stained platform. The walls surrounding the platform were black too, as was the chimney. It had a brick floor and a beautiful, perfectly round, brick well on the other side of a wall. Anyone standing inside the kitchen could draw water from the well from a big window. I opened the window and looked down into the well for a closer look, and was again struck by the perfection of its shape. It was indeed deep, the bricks perfectly placed and aligned. A pulley hung just over my head and my elbows were resting on a wide ledge on which, in the old days, there would have been a bucket attached to a thick coir rope.

By the kitchen were tiny rooms fitted with massive stones, for grinding and pounding. Two of the rooms had huge, shoulder-high chests made of heavy teak. The musty smell of grain still hung in the air.

The back of the house had a big porch that opened into a yard, which was bursting with colours. Bougainvillea — red, orange, white and pink — grew wild along the pillars of the porch, up the trunks of trees and along the low walls that divided the yard. Bougainvillea everywhere! The colours all mixed up. The yard hadn't been cleared for decades but hidden among the giant weeds and long grass and dead *peepul* leaves, I detected *tulsi*, papaya, pepper, henna, *kadi patta*, and several varieties of jasmine and hibiscus.

From the porch, one could see for miles around — the entire hillside and the river that flowed at the foot of the hill. There was a small wooden gate to the side of the yard. One could open the gate and walk down shallow stone steps to the river. The steps had a protective tiled awning, covered with bougainvillea. The gate was jammed in the mud and weeds and I couldn't open it to go down to the river.

That was my first glimpse of the river. My *puzha*. She was muddy and swollen because of the rains and looked like a swift-flowing stream of tea. She flowed purposefully, as if she was late for an important board meeting. She seemed to be saying she was happy to see me but she couldn't stop right then — there'd be plenty of time afterwards. And she was right.

Also in the backyard was a bathing tank, a most fascinating piece of architecture. Especially for me, fresh from Bombay where we were lucky if we had ten square inches to bathe in. As I stood facing it, all I could see was a wall with a hole in it, and a door. Inside, to my left, was the bathing area. The hole outside was for heating a large, almost giant, pot of water that one could access from inside the bathroom. I stood there imagining maids scurrying up and down the whole day with water from the well, ensuring that there was always enough hot water in the bath. The maid need not have entered the bath since the pot was half inside and half outside the wall. The bathing area was so ingeniously laid out that smoke from the fire that burned under the pot could not have entered the bathroom. After a nice hot bath, one could go for a swim down the stone steps to the tank, which was about the size of a swimming pool. On that day, the water was dirty and smelly. But it didn't require much imagination to picture it clean and sparkling in the sunlight, reflecting the fronds of the nearby coconut trees.

At the far end of the yard — actually called a *thodi*, if you want the accurate terminology — was a *peepul* tree whose boughs formed a rustling green canopy for the idols of snakes beneath. Most *tharavaats* had similar shrines. For the Snake Gods and the Gods of the elements. The mud idols had fallen down and lay scattered — faint traces of *haldi* and *kum kum* still visible. I reached down involuntarily and brushed aside the dead leaves with my hand, straightening the idols. I didn't know how to arrange them, so I put the biggest one in the centre and the smaller ones on either side. I stood there for a while, looking at them, trying to feel something. Something devotional, you know. But I didn't feel anything.

There were other broken-down structures to the side of the house, behind the *pathaipera* — the granary — the ruin I had briefly mistaken to be Alanghat. I deduced that the other ruins must have been the carriage-house and the stables.

As I walked the considerable distance back to the house, I found it difficult to imagine that this place had been the scene of a ghastly tragedy. (What that tragedy was, I didn't know. My parents had never spoken of it and I had no other relatives whom I could ask.) The place was peaceful and picturesque; and yet the house had an air of gloom about it. If it had eyes, they would have had a grief-stricken look.

Two broad wooden staircases on either side of the front porch lead up to the first floor. There were smaller, steeper ones inside too. The roof of the front porch formed a verandah for the first floor. A tiled roof that had the most exquisite woodwork I have ever seen covered this verandah. All the windows in the house had shutters made of teak. They hung crazily on their hinges, warped, bleached and bloated out of shape. At one time, they must have been so well polished that they must have gleamed in the sun.

~

I spent that morning trying to imagine myself sleeping there alone at night, with no one but those portraits for company. Those eyes. By evening, strange objects would throw strange shadows, the wind would howl and the steps would creak ... .

I stopped trying to imagine any further. I knew I would be petrified if I were alone there at night. I am Indian and I know as much about *havelis* and *dak bunglas* as the next person. And yes, *Madhumati* frightened me.

Discretion being, as they say, the better part of valor, I asked Binkity if I could stay another night at his place. I didn't feel too comfortable doing that. After all, I didn't know him too well. But I didn't know what else to do. He was pretty decent about it though.

However, I changed my mind as we were driving out. The nagging feeling that it would not be right to spend another night at Binkity's place was growing stronger. On an impulse, I decided to look for Nandakumar's house. After all, he was at least a kinsman.

He turned out to be my nearest neighbour! He had an old-fashioned house at the bottom of the hill. The front door was divided into four. It took the lady who answered my 'Anybody there?' quite some time to open all of them. Nandakumar was there. And he hadn't received my father's letter. In fact, the first ten minutes were quite confusing because I assumed that he had received it and for some reason hadn't been able to come to the station. He, on the other hand, couldn't figure out who the hell I was!

Nandakumar was a quiet person. His wife, Shailaja, the person who had opened the door, was just the opposite. Talkative and bubbly. They had two small children — Amit and Sumit. Nandu

was an insurance agent. He also owned a grocery store (remember
Nandu inte kada?) near the bus-stand in Kunnathur, with a pay
phone booth. Within minutes of sorting out the confusion, I found
myself sitting next to Binkity, in Nandakumar's small and crammed
dining room, it's low windowsill full of steel *dabbas* and bottles
arranged neatly in rows. The room smelled vaguely of something,
but I didn't know what. A smell that most village homes have.

We had tea and banana chips, talking as if we had known each
other for years, the rain pattering outside. Behind the door, Amit
and Sumit played a sort of peek-a-boo game with me, screaming
with excitement whenever I caught them peeping.

I was relieved that they had turned out to be such likable people,
and that we had instantly liked each other. I did not hesitate in
moving into their house the same afternoon.

~

*N*andakumar's house was a long structure built in a low-lying
area. A huge *peepul* tree canopied the house and rustled in the
wind and rain all night long, providing the background score to
my thoughts during those long, sleepless nights.

The walls of the house were covered with pictures of Gods and
Godesses — the Gods looking like Goddesses and the Goddesses
looking like Hema Malini. Vishnu was well represented, so was
Lakshmi and Saraswati and Subramanyam. There were smaller
pictures too — each one with a story. Hanuman flying with a

40

mountain held aloft on a finger, a saint dreaming of Krishna, Shiva carrying his dead wife on his shoulder with his third eye open. They were all there. Everywhere.

The *puja* room itself had twenty-six portraits. The twenty-sixth was a massive *Guruvayurappan*. It had the place of honour — right in the centre, behind the lamp, and consequently got the biggest rose or the biggest hibiscus from the garden. The others had to be content with either jasmine, or *mandiyarvattom*, or even a sprig of *tulsi*. I couldn't help apologizing to the other Gods each time I placed a rose on a *Guruvayurappan*. By the time I reached the last one — a small *Ayappan* hidden behind the door — I'd be distinctly uncomfortable because by then my flower basket would be empty, except for some *tulsi*. Within a week of taking over this job from Shailaja, I had developed a complicated rota to ensure an equitable distribution of my offerings to the deities.

~

*B*y the end of the first week, I had slipped into a routine. Shailaja had become a good friend and I had had my first long-distance quarrel with my mother. It was our first long-distance quarrel — not our first quarrel. That must have taken place when I was about a week old. My mother and I quarreled all the time. Anything could lead to a quarrel, but the quarrel itself was always about one thing — me and my ways and she and her ways. We didn't approve of each other's ways. I thought my mother was childish and incapable of loving anyone. She thought that I was inconsiderate, impractical, and that I lacked character. I blamed her for my desperate need to be loved — to be told repeatedly that I was loved — but not once did she ever tell me that. My earliest memories are of her pushing me out of the way or ignoring me. Though she infuriated me and there were times when I hated her, I still hung around, unable to live without her, returning to her after each fight only to feel more frustrated and furious. But returning anyway. Waiting and hoping for something, I couldn't quite comprehend.

If I had to give one reason for leaving Bombay, I'd say it was the mass of overpowering and contradictory feelings that I felt for my mother, all of which were knotted up inside me, tearing me apart.

I needed space to breathe and to unravel myself. And I couldn't do it with her around. She'd help me up with one hand and clobber me down with the other. I had begun to feel that I had to get away from her if I ever wanted to be whole again.

~

*T*he phone conversation began cordially enough. I told them about Alanghat and my experience at Cheriathur station. In turn, they told me that they had finally sold our flat in Worli, and that they would soon be sending me the money to renovate Alanghat.

My parents had moved to Bombay in 1950. The wisest thing

they did was to have bought two flats. One in Worli in 1959, and the other in Juhu, in 1968. We had given the Worli flat on rent as soon as we bought it; and of course couldn't get it back because of that old Rent Control thing. But by a stroke of luck (for us), our tenant, Mrs. Mudaliar, died suddenly. She had been long-widowed and her children had gone away to Australia at the very first opportunity they got. A thing that most sensible children do. Only idiots like me stay behind.

My father took advantage of the confusion that followed her death and took possession of the flat. That was in 1977. I lived in that flat for eight years after that, and that was the flat my father had just sold.

My parents live in the Juhu flat. We moved in there in 1971, when I was sixteen. Before that, we had lived in Colaba in a rented flat in a building called Rashid Mansions, close to the Wodehouse Club. That's neither here nor there, really. Just thought I'd tell you because if you're familiar with Bombay, you might know the place. It's an old building that should have collapsed ages ago.

~

*B*ack to my story now: my father had heard that there were many rich Muslim families keen on buying houses like Alanghat — they were status symbols, you know! So he thought that if we got the place done up a bit, so that it didn't scare anybody away, we might be able to sell it and rid ourselves of it. I had jumped at the chance and had volunteered to oversee the renovation. An excuse, of course, to flee from Bombay. I needed an excuse because I didn't have the money to just pack a case and leave. In any case, I didn't want to hurt my father by walking out. I didn't tell him then that I had no intention of returning ever again.

The quarrel started just as I was about to hang up. My mother, who had never approved of the idea right from the start, insisted that I leave Kunnathur. She said that if I didn't want to return to Bombay it was okay; I could get a job in Palakkad as a teacher but *under no circumstances* — a favorite phrase, a phrase that never failed to get my hackles up — was I to remain in Kunnathur. It was my mother's long-standing and dearest wish that I become a teacher. The fact that I absolutely loathed the prospect was completely irrelevant.

Just as I was about to hang up she said that my father was going to write to someone they knew in Palakkad to get me a job in a school there. And so we quarreled. But because we had fought this particular quarrel a thousand times before, we were well rehearsed and it finished pretty quickly. It also finished quickly because I banged down the phone, cutting her off mid-sentence.

I sat there and fumed. Angry enough to wreck the phone and set Nandu's shop on fire. When would she understand? I was beginning to feel she never would. All our lives we'd be like railway tracks, always together yet always apart. Apart because she wanted it that way.

Three

Karkitakam Sankramam

*F*or the last five days, the skies had scowled menacingly down at us. The days were sullen and overcast and the rain pelted us night and day.

Nandu's house was in a low-lying area and we would have been marooned had it not been for the huge tank that had been dug behind the house a generation ago, to catch rainwater. Since everyone seemed stoical about it, I too learnt to become stoical. It rained quite heavily in Bombay too, but there the elements were not quite so aggressive, if you know what I mean. Nandu's house was remote and isolated — a Wuthering Heights kind of place — and when the wind howled, it... well, it certainly *howled*! But this was apparently normal. It was supposed to be like this. The first day - the *Sankramam* - of the month of *Karkitakam* was the day of heaviest rain. It was preceded by the *vaave*, the new moon. So this was expected. Dry or merely wet weather would have been an aberration. This deluge was normal.

Shailaja and I sat on the steps of the porch every evening, bitten by mosquitoes and watching the rain. The conversation was remarkably prosaic.

'The potatoes are getting spoiled.'

'All right then, we'll have potatoes for dinner and finish them. Better go buy some vegetables tomorrow. That old man — *Aa kazhavan* — has stopped coming with his basket. Is he dead? *Chatuvo*?'

'Must have stopped coming because of the rain.'

'Aah, yes. *Paavam* - poor thing.'

All the electricity poles had collapsed a long time ago, and we'd forgotten that there was such a thing as electricity. Every evening, we'd light the big brass oil lamps placed on the floor in the corners of the front rooms. The bedrooms had no lamps. We just had to grope about until we found our way. Thinking back, those were the nice days. My tired brain felt soothed and I could feel myself unwinding.

Sometimes, when the rain let up for a while, we went up the hill to Alanghat and walked around the place, imagining what things were like a hundred years ago, making elaborate plans for the renovation that was to start when *Karkitakam* was over and *Chingam* began. The ease with I had slipped into thinking in terms of the Malayalam calendar amazed me. According to the English calendar, I was planning to begin work sometime in the middle of

August. By then, monsoon would be on the wane and we would have long spells of sunshine. *Chingam* was the harvest month, the month of *Onam*. An auspicious time to begin work on Alanghat.

It was on one such visit to Alanghat that we went to the Alanghat family temple. We were walking through the *thodi,* our voices resounding in the silence that always seemed to envelop Alanghat. We had walked to the very end and were turning back when I first saw the temple. I had missed it on my first visit.

Clutching at each other, we walked through a gap in the low wall and up the path that led to the temple. The place was desolate, and the temple was black with moss and fungus. It was built under the biggest *peepul* tree I had ever seen in my life — each of its thick and arched boughs capable of being a separate tree in itself. We stopped at another low wall surrounding the temple precincts, too scared to go any further. This was an unfrequented *devi*-temple and both of us were familiar with enough folklore to feel terrified at the thought of incurring the wrath of the *devi*, her curses heaped on us for not looking after her temple. So we stood there, our hands cold and clammy, looking fearfully around, expecting anything to happen.

When nothing did, I gathered all my courage and walked up to the entrance of the temple and was about to step inside when I saw snakes. It seemed as if there were hundreds of them. A pit full. Teeming and coiling and slithering. I put my hand on the pillar to steady myself as I climbed the broken steps, and I felt something move under it. I snatched it back and stood there, unable to move.

The slithering and uncoiling stopped and I saw that there was actually a single snake. A huge one. I stared at it, horrified, rooted to the spot like a *peepul* tree. So frightened that I couldn't move. We stood like that — face to face — the snake and I — for what seemed like the rest of my life; until somehow, I willed my legs to move and with a massive effort turned around and ran, my knees barely holding me up and my throat dry. I reached Shailaja and pulled her by the arm, gasping, *Aiyo, Shailaja Odikyo, Odikyo*! Shailaja run, run!

She screamed loudly, bringing the rain that had been hanging ominously overhead, down on us like a waterfall. We both ran screaming hysterically all the way back to her house. The trailing creepers and long grass made me bounce even more. I ran trying not to touch the ground, and did not stop until we were safely inside. We sat one the ledge in the porch, gasping for breath, our sides aching. We were both dripping like drenched rats. Only then did she shake my knee and ask, 'But what happened? Why were we running?'

That night as I lay in bed reliving that incident, I remembered the snake's body language as we had stood staring at each other. It had looked startled. Frightened to death. We had frightened each other to death! I'm sure it had run away too. As fast as its ribs could take it.

Nandu and Shailaja showed a lot of interest in Alanghat and my plans for it. As though it was their own house. I felt vaguely ashamed at the way I had thought of them as "distantly related"!

Nandu's father, Parameshwaran, had belonged to *Vattavompaday*, the same clan as Keshavan Nair, my great-grandfather. That's how we were related in terms of the family tree. He had lived in Kunnathur for years and years and my mother had given him the keys of Alanghat entrusting him with its upkeep — a job which he had done faithfully and to the best of his ability until he died in 1979. All those years he had been just a name to me. I never read the letters and the long financial statements that arrived regularly by post. How was I to know then that the house, the place and the people, who had sounded so remote and unfamiliar to me for so many years, would one day become dearer to me than everything else? Had I known at that time, I would have thanked Parameshwaran from the bottom of my heart for not just looking after Alanghat, but also for preserving it.

There is a black and white photograph of him in Nandu's house. I looked at it sometimes, wondering about all the things he would have been able to tell me about the mystery that was Alanghat. I knew that everybody in Kunnathur knew more than I did, but I didn't feel comfortable asking anyone; not even Nandu and Shailaja who, by now, were family in the real sense of the word and not just because of the family tree.

~

I was beginning to recognise quite a few people in Kunnathur now. Most of them had called on me, either individually or in a

49

group. They were all small landowners and all of them dressed identically. The men wore white shirts and white *mundus* and after dark, all of them carried big steel torches. The women wore off-white *mundus*, with a coloured line — *kara* — running down the edge. Their blouses were the same colour as the *kara.* Some of the younger women wore nylon, wash-and-wear sarees.

I could see curiosity written all over their faces. Why had this girl come and opened up a house that had been locked up for a quarter of a century? And with that, she had also revived all the old gossip and memories of the strange, tragic happenings that were linked to the house.

There was another angle too. Time had by no means stood still in Kunnathur. Things had changed. New equations of power had evolved. Would she upset the apple cart? Could she? The women, I knew, were more interested in my personal life. How old was I? Why wasn't I married? What was I going to do here all alone? Why had I left Bombay to come here, of all places? I could hear these questions buzzing around Kunnathur like a swarm of bees. I pretended I was unaffected by the gossip and that it didn't bother me in the least. I wanted to believe that if I left trouble alone, it would, in turn, leave me alone. I didn't want to be dragged into a controversy. I only wanted to be left alone. Would they leave me alone? If I pulled rank, maybe they would. After all, I belonged to the 'aristocracy', and I was rich. If the first didn't mean anything any more, surely the second did. I could make them do whatever I wanted. I had never been so calculating before and it shocked me.

It was as if an ugly monster had suddenly leapt out of nowhere. I didn't know that side of me even existed.

Anyway, I had started recognising people by then. There was V.K. Menon, there was Dr. Krishnankutty, there was Radhabai Amma, there was C.K.P. Nambiar (known as *Soap Chandran* because he had worked for Lifebuoy), there was *Ice Mani*, the owner of the ice-factory and there was Nanikutty Amma, an old widow, known as *African Ammuma* (pronounced *gafreekyun*) because she had lived in British East Africa for nearly forty years.

Then, there was M. Shankaran Nair - Muthote Shankaran Nair - the *Panchaayat* President and the pillar of Cheriathur society, the man who decided that he hated me even before he had set eyes on me.

~

*N*andu and Shailaja led very quiet lives, seldom going anywhere except to the temple. They had almost no friends their age as Kunnathur was a village full of old people. The only people they visited regularly were Solomon and Saramma, an elderly couple. They were Pentecost Christians and they lived in Manuthy, a two-hour drive from Kunnathur. Nandu and Shailaja visited them every Saturday evening. Religiously. All four of them would dress up — the children in *Baba Suits*, Shailaja in a neatly draped nylon sari, her face white with talcum powder and Nandu in a bush shirt and trousers — and march off to the bus stand to wait for the bus to Manuthy, and return only after sunset. They also talked about Solomon and Saramma very often and never did anything without first consulting them. So much so that even though I had never met Solomon and Saramma, I felt as if I knew both of them very well.

Because Nandu and Shailaja led such quiet lives and had few visitors, I was protected from the curiosity of the villagers who, after the initial excitement, let me be. For which I was most grateful.

~

*T*he day the road-transport-company's truck arrived with the rest of my belongings and my vehicle — a ramshackle Trax. I had despatched the rest of my things by road, before leaving Bombay and I hadn't told my parents. No sense in getting them worked up. I started driving around almost immediately, exploring Kunnathur and the places nearby. I even followed that arrow pointing heavenwards until I reached Edavannur, and further ahead till Thripallur; sometimes getting caught in the rain and being stranded for hours.

It was on one such ill-fated jaunt that I found the *Shiva Kshetram* in Thripallur. Shiva and I have had a long and turbulent relationship, spread over many lives. Mine of course, not his.

It had suddenly started raining so heavily that I couldn't see anything ahead of me and had to pull up to the side of the road. I could see a building outlined a little ahead of me and I made a dash towards it. It turned out to be a beautiful old temple — almost forgotten by time. The temple was in an inner square that was open to the sky. I sat in the protected entrance, on a broad stone platform, and watched the raindrops shatter themselves on the granite slabs in the courtyard.

As I sat there, my mind wandered over to my past. My childhood. School. The double life I had led. At school I was popular — the life of the party — but at home I was silent and morose. Yet, I had hated school and loved home.

After wandering all over the place and making due halts at the compulsory ports of call — my mother and Vivek — it finally stopped at the thing that had caused me the greatest pain and confusion for years. My music.

I had started learning *carnatic* music at the age of five, on my mother's insistence. A *bhagvathar* was found and I started learning the *veena* and singing. The *bhagavathar* would come thrice a week, at six o'clock sharp, and I would be ready and waiting, with my hair oiled and plaited, and wearing a *pavadai* - long skirt - and blouse stitched especially for the occasion. I showed 'great promise' and the *bhagavathar* was 'very happy' with me. Each time he uttered those two phrases, I would puff up a little. Gradually, I developed a different personality, one that I reserved for all occasions. I began to talk in soft, mellifluous tones and when I felt somebody was watching, I treated the *veena* with exaggerated respect. By the time I was ten, I had made a name for myself in school and in the local Malayali Association as a "child prodigy".

By the time I was thirteen, I was a pompous, over-confident, conceited brat in need of a tight slap.

When I turned seventeen, something happened to me. Suddenly, I couldn't bear to look at the *veena*. I hated to sing and I hated the *bhagavathar*. I would pick a quarrel with my mother and storm out of the house on the days I had a lesson, returning only when I was sure the *bhagavathar* had left. I became unpleasant and rude, and soon my parents stopped the lessons. I could sense that my mother was relieved and that made me angrier. I felt she couldn't bear to see me being good at anything.

My seventeenth year was a rebellious one. I rebelled against everything. My animosity against my mother, seething inside me for so long, erupted like a volcano. I wouldn't listen to a thing she said. I stopped studying and began staying out the whole day. It was a sort of anti-establishment phase. Those years were like that. Anybody who was in their teens during the early seventies will know what I'm talking about. There was a wild restlessness in the air. A claustrophobia. A frustration. And in my case, of course, there was the hatred I felt towards my mother.

~

*D*espite all this, music did not reject me. It went on playing in my head as if it had a will of it's own, a will that was much stronger than mine. When it grew too loud to ignore, I picked up my *veena* and played it. But that was the only time I played. Not otherwise.

After some time, the music in my head became muffled, as if there was a glass partition between us. I could see it but couldn't touch it. I felt estranged from it. When I opened my mouth to sing, I sounded pathetic — as if the sound was coming from my throat without the consent of my soul. There was no resonance, no reverberations within me. My playing became so desultory and mechanical that it sounded like a Maruti in reverse gear. After a while, I stopped trying. The loss became a huge thorn, embedded deep in my heart, causing a constant ache; an ache that, along with all the other feelings and emotions, I had chosen to ignore.

~

I don't know for how long I sat alone in the temple, with nothing but my thoughts for company. It was only when I realised the rain had eased that I got up and started walking towards my Trax. There was a huge *peepul* tree outside the temple. I stopped to look at it. The wind was playing havoc with its leaves, tossing them around violently and mercilessly. But they still hung on, firm in the knowledge that the storm would pass. Just as I was hanging on, believing that after winter there would be spring. My great-grandmother had said so.

Four

The promised draft took twelve days to arrive. There was a letter with it, from my mother, condemning me for hanging up on her and explaining to me in full detail the meaning of the word "character". It made me grit my teeth with irritation. Her ability to make me feel worthless was remarkable. My father had written a short note too. Just to tell me that the paperwork for the sale of the flat was over and the buyers had taken possession.

I was glad that I had finally got rid of the Worli flat. I had moved there a year after I got a job with The Economic Times and had lived there for eight years. I had left Juhu after a blazing row with my mother about the way I had arranged the flowers in the *puja* room. Arranging flowers in the *puja* room had been my favourite job since the time I was a little child, and she knew that. That's what hurt. It hurt so much that I never went anywhere near the *puja* room again. Till Kunnathur.

She had been sitting there watching me arrange a *mala* of jasmine around one of the pictures. Just then my father walked in and she turned to him and said, 'She's arranged the flowers as if they were a crown of thorns.' Seems silly now but at that time it wasn't silly at all. I left the house two days later, hating her so much that I never wanted to see her face again.

I moved to a paying guest accommodation at Peddar Road. It was a large room with an attached bathroom, a private entrance and a microscopic garden — part of a large ground-floor flat. The owners were a rich Bengali couple with a son who was twenty-eight years old and mentally retarded. He was a huge fellow, gentle most of the time but once in a while he'd get out of hand and then he was terrifying. His family had got him married to a poor orphan girl in the hope that he'd suddenly cease to be retarded after marriage. I never could understand that. What he needed was medical attention and a trained nurse. But no! All Indian mothers tend to think that whatever is wrong with their precious sons would vanish the second they got them married.

Anyway, they installed him and his wife in the apartment on Peddar Road and one of his brothers came occasionally to check on them. They were the people who I negotiated with before moving in but I paid the rent to Usha, the orphan. I felt sorry for her. She was scared stiff of her husband's family but she had nowhere else to go, and since her husband needed constant attention, she couldn't so much as step out of the house. The house was dark and dingy and unfurnished — not a "home" at all. She had no visitors and no friends. The neighbours kept to themselves and so did her paying guest! Poor thing — life was hell for her.

About a year after I moved in, our tenant in the Worli flat, Mrs. Mudaliar suddenly died and my father took possession of the flat. I was secretly relieved. Being independent and headstrong was all very well but I hadn't slept properly for a year now because the thought of that man breaking down my door in one of his rages petrified me, keeping me awake.

Two things happened in January 1978. Two things which would forever change the course of my life. Well, three actually — if you count the fact that it was then that I moved into the Worli flat. The first thing was that Vivek joined The Economic Times and I fell in love with him, in the classic fashion. Head over heels. And the second thing was that I had a flaming row with my mother for sending my horoscope and photograph in response to a matrimonial advertisement in the newspaper. That flaming row had been the mother of all flaming rows. It was a fight that we haven't forgotten even today; that's how vicious it was.

~

*L*ooking back, I suppose I could have done things differently. Perhaps if I had allowed my parents to "do their duty", I would have been married now, with two children. "Has your maid come today, Mrs. Nambiar?/Mrs. Nair?/Mrs. Menon?" I rolled the names on my tongue, trying to get the right flavour. But I couldn't get it. It just wasn't me. I was too. I couldn't imagine just fitting into a role. I couldn't lay aside my individuality, my identity and don another's. An Indian marriage can be a rather traumatic for women. It's like dying and being reborn. The only difference is that in the new birth you still remember your past life but have no claim on it. All personal ambitions, goals — even beliefs — have to be sacrificed at the altar of marriage. You are not expected that you do it willingly for the man you love — if at all you know him enough to love him. It is expected of you as your duty towards the marriage. In "modern" marriages it is worse because the bitter lozenge is sugar coated. Life is so difficult for today's woman, because she is neither here nor there. Her parents educate her, she takes up a job, she is allowed to have a dream; but all that is only *till*... . When a "good match" comes along, she must suddenly revert to Indian Womanhood — not take up too much space and accommodate everybody. In one sense, the old days were better. Kinder. There were no lies. There was only one way and a girl had to follow that.

No, there was no way I could be a Mrs. Menon or a Mrs. Nambiar or a Mrs. whatever. But how do I explain Vivek? What plausible excuse can there be for falling in love with a man in the knowledge that he is already married? There isn't any and I won't pretend otherwise. And why should there be? Does everything have to be justified? Does one love only when it is socially proper to do so? Is love "morally" right only when the society stamps it with its seal of approval.

But society changes its moral code, doesn't it? *Doesn't it?* Didn't a man have more than one wife not so long ago? It was the proper thing to do then. How then has it become so outrageous and immoral now, when all the other norms have remained the same? Or is it the feminist angle? *How can you do this to another woman?* As if I have the power to actually *do* something to someone else! What I find very difficult to explain yet is so important to understand is that it was not something I did out of choice. It was not deliberate. I did not choose that man because he was married and so that I could *do this* to his wife. Why would I? I was a slave to my own inadequacy, of that fatal need to be loved. If I had a choice, if I were in a position to choose, I might have chosen differently.

In any case, the fact that he was married was never the issue. I never expected him to leave his wife and I never asked him to. All I wanted was to be with him. Whatever part of him I could get — for whatever time — was enough. The first time I saw him, I felt drawn towards him. It was spontaneous. I liked him, and that is what was important. Underlying the love — which was like a tidal wave — was this liking. It is important to *like* a person, isn't it? No matter how he or she may be related to you. It is such a basic thing.

Anyway, I liked him tremendously. Everything about him felt right. His manner, his voice, his hands. Everything. He excited me and I wasn't at all surprised when we started spending more and more time together. It seemed very natural. As if that was the way it had to be. I knew — of course, I did — that it was a relationship with no future for me. But at that time, it didn't matter. The attraction — the magnet — was too strong. And we grew so close to each other, that I couldn't imagine him hurting or ever leaving me.

But to be perfectly honest, those eight years were agony. Even the pleasure was agonizing. Instead of setting me free, the fact that I had no claim on him made me cling on to him even more. Consequently, I was always either experiencing a very high high or an abysmally low low. I suppose that should have warned me. That absolute lack of control over my emotional wellbeing should have warned me; should have prepared me for the way thing were going to turn out. But what is the point in reminiscing? All said and done — inevitable or not — I was devastated when he left me. The pain I then felt has now faded but the memory never will. *Debris*.

I remember the way my mother had pleaded with me, scolded me — even blackmailed me. She had used every technique in the book — and some of her own, ingenuous ones — to get me to leave him. But I couldn't. I knew she was right, but I just couldn't do it. I needed him desperately. Actually, my feelings towards my mother were at their most positive during that time. He made me feel good about myself and so she no longer had the power to make me feel worthless, as though she hated me.

But when he left, I turned to her. And I know that I would never have made if it hadn't been for her. She was compassionate about the whole thing and was genuinely grieving for me.

Our personal hatred continued, however.

Five

*T*here is a place in Bombay called Matunga. It is known as the city's mini Kerala. In fact, you can live there without knowing any language other than Malayalam. It has its own temples with Malayali priests, its own vegetable shops which sell the kind of vegetables Malayalis like, jewellery stores with traditional Malayali ornaments, shops that sell "set *mundu*s" and towels — everything a Malayali would need. Matunga also has a famous *nadi shastra* astrologer. People go to him to consult him for everything. At least they did then. He is probably dead now. A prospective groom's horoscope, a prospective bride's horoscope, career prospects, births, deaths, health, building a house … he always seemed to know what was wrong and what could be done to rectify it. My mother used to visit him too and I would tag along because he said such intriguing things. According to him, I am not supposed to die until I am ninety-five. I believe it. Something deep down tells me that it's true and that is why I was so determined to put that whole Vivek thing behind me. Sixty-five years — more, I think — would be a long time to live brooding over another woman's husband.

There was a time — after my fourth abortion in eight years — when I had seriously considered killing myself. Not that Vivek ever insisted I have them. Actually the issue was never discussed. I just went ahead and had one each time I found myself pregnant, because I was so scared I'd lose him. Which I eventually did.

Vivek phoned the day before and told me that we would have to end our relationship. For months afterwards, I used to force myself to repeat his words, over and over again. Like feeling a wound twenty times a day just to see if it hurts, knowing that it does. He said — let me get it right — yes, he said, 'I think we should call it off now. Enough is enough.'

It didn't hurt just now, when I wrote that. But back then, it seared a hole right through me. That was all I could think of when I lay in the hospital bed, with nothing on but the funny robe they give you to wear. The nurse who was cleaning me didn't look at my face. Not even once. I think I was just another hole for her. The tears never stopped, not when I was wheeled away. Not when I was in pre-op. Not even when I was on the operating table. The doctor was kind. He spoke very nicely to the hole before I went under.

I stayed at the hospital until evening and then I took a taxi to my flat. Sitting there in my room, I seriously contemplated ending my life. That was the first time I felt the terrible restlessness and torment that later became so familiar to me. I sat alone in that room, too miserable to get up and switch on the light. I just sat and cried. I don't remember having cried like that before or since. It was almost a wail — hoarse and ugly.

I lay awake that entire night. My neck ached with tension, my fingers felt stiff and my eyes felt gritty and they burned but I couldn't sleep. Desperate thoughts went through my head and underlying all that was the desire to die.

The next morning, I didn't want to get up. It was a working day but I just didn't feel up to it. I lay in bed the whole day. I was still crying and had started using a bed-sheet to blow my nose because my handkerchief was inadequate. Towards afternoon, I felt terribly hungry but I couldn't get up and cook something. Every nerve in me waited for him to phone or ring the doorbell. But he didn't. Nobody came to see me and nobody phoned.

Night fell. The thought of spending another sleepless night was unbearable, so I crawled out of bed and hunted through my medicine cupboard until I found a strip of Valium. My mother used to take half a tablet at night, every once in a while, and had left it behind on one of her earlier visits. I swallowed four.

I had horrible nightmares that night. I dreamt that my arm fell off and that I was hunting frantically for it all over the place. The broken stump of my shoulder was vivid in the dream but it didn't hurt when the arm fell off. There was no blood and no pain. Just this frantic search for it all over the house. The fear was what made this whole thing such a nightmare. For some reason, I couldn't walk straight. I lurched from side to side, with the broken stump on my shoulder hanging before me. I don't remember if I dreamt this all night long but I was certainly relieved when morning came at last.

The awful nightmare didn't stop me from taking two more valiums before going to work that day. I was a bundle of nerves. I wanted to meet Vivek — talk to him — and somehow put an end to this misery. By the time I reached the office, I was so restless that I couldn't sit still at my desk. My hand reached for the phone every second. I called Tara, my friend and colleague, but her line was busy. I was too tense and agitated to hang up and wait, so I kept trying over and over again. But I couldn't get through. Then I called my mother. When I heard her voice, I hung up and tried Tara's number again. Busy.

I knew that what I really wanted to do was to call Vivek. But I could not. I sat there and smoked. Cigarette after cigarette after cigarette. When Thambi, our office boy, came with the first round of coffee, I grabbed a cup. Not because I wanted it but because I needed something to do.

I couldn't concentrate on anything. Around me, the office was filling up. People were joking or laughing; or hanging up their jackets and putting away their helmets. A week ago, I would have been right there in the centre of things, but that day I cowered at my desk and hoped that everybody would leave me alone. However, they didn't. How were they to know? So I chatted and laughed. Or at least I went through the motions. My mouth went dry and my cheek muscles ached. I began perspiring profusely. At one point, there was a lull in the general banter and only my voice could be heard. It sounded thin and awful and I faltered when I heard myself talk. I saw Tara walk up to me and knew instinctively that she was going to tell me something I wouldn't be able to handle. I cringed inside.

But I couldn't stop it from coming. Vivek had gone on annual leave. The whole family had gone to Delhi. His wife's parents were there. *The whole family* sans mistress. Mistress is not family. She is the bitch, the home breaker.

He would be away for a month. I felt sick in the pit of my stomach and my throat began to ache and throb. I have no clue as to what I did in office the whole day. I don't think I did anything. Tara stopped by every now and then. She has a loud, booming foghorn sort of voice and I remember her trying to whisper in my ear, most unsuccessfully, that I looked terrible and couldn't I please act as if everything was okay?

Finally, at 5.30 I found myself huddled and miserable in Tara's Maruti as she drove back to Worli. Tara talked about this and that. I could tell she was worried about me. Worried about what I might do. She kept asking me to 'say something'. Today when I think about it, it makes me smile. But that day, her 'say something' yanked me back from the mouth of a black cave — a cave I didn't want to leave.

She was good to me those lousy weeks. We'd drive around or

walk down Worli Seaface. She didn't mind my talking of nothing but Vivek. I remember one evening very clearly. We were walking down the Seaface, enjoying the breeze and I was telling her about some book I was trying to read on the importance of prayer. I was telling her that maybe we led such roller-coaster lives because we didn't pray enough. And that perhaps if we fasted and prayed, sang *bhajans*, learnt Sanskrit and read the *Vedas* we'd lead more peaceful lives. In the middle of all this, I suddenly remembered that her altar at home was out in the balcony for want of space. So I said, 'But Tara, your God's out in your balcony'. She stopped in the middle of the road, completely oblivious of everybody else and yelled, 'Yeah, that's why I'm in the wilderness!'

Tara was mad. A raving lunatic. Mad in a nice sort of way. Like the "crazy ball" children play with these days. You could never tell what she was going to do next. Even she couldn't tell. I never could fathom why she took up journalism, of all things. She should have been a gypsy clairvoyant or something exotic like that. Not because of her looks — she was a breathtaking beauty. It was her whole approach to life. Sort of mystical and other-worldly. For her, life was not about being practical — about getting dinner or about cleaning the fans. It was a distant purple mountain shrouded in swirling mist. The dinner and the fans and the rest of it somehow got done but it was the mountain that constantly beckoned. It was its mysterious promise that kept her going.

~

*B*y the end of the week the whole office had figured that the great romance had soured. Or maybe they didn't have to figure it. Maybe my face said it all. I don't know. The days crawled by, each minute a burden — a dead weight. I waited expectantly for the third of March. That is when he was to return, and I would talk to him. Beg him to take me back. I don't remember bathing or cooking or eating or combing my hair or doing any work that entire month. I only remember taking those valiums every two hours. And I remember the feverish urgency, the anxiety and the desperate hope that drove me relentlessly — that burned me in its raging fire.

It didn't work out that way though. On the second of the month, he went to Tara's place and asked her to reason with me. He told her to ask me to behave like a lady. He told her that he respected me and that he'd always be my friend but he could never be with me again. He said he loved his wife passionately and couldn't bear to hurt her. He wanted to end our relationship before she decided to do something, like file for a divorce. It's so funny, you know. Sometimes I wonder what would have happened if she had filed for divorce. Would I have married Vivek? Would he have asked me to? Would we have been happy together? I have all the answers now, half a lifetime later. Yes, I would have married him. No, he would not have asked me to marry him. And no, we would not have been happy together. Bingo!

~

Tara told him that I was in a bad state because of the abortion and all the rest of it. She wondered if it was the right time for all this. And then he said something I will never understand — not as long as I live. He said, 'Oh, that was not my baby. None of them were. She has always had multiple partners.'

So, the third of March turned out to be the day I resigned from The Economic Times, after working there for nine years. And the third of March also turned out to be the day I swallowed 57 valiums.

Six

But I didn't die. Thank God for that! That's why I believe what the *nadi shastra* man in Matunga had to say. If you are destined to live, you will. Even if I had swallowed 507 valiums, I'd have lived. Probably crapped out quantities of black stuff the next day, but I'd have lived. Destiny.

I woke up in the hospital and the first thing I saw was my mother's face. Tired. Ashen. Old. I didn't have what it took to look into her eyes, so I looked away. I could hear my father's voice as he talked to the nurse. I noticed the feeble ring to it for the first time in my life. He was getting on in years too. There is no way I can describe the terrible guilt I felt lying there in that hospital bed.

A long time ago, a friend of mine was telling me how he had started doing drugs, while at college. Things got so bad that his father had to come and take him back home. He was all skin and bone — quite a mess, he said. But he got okay after a while and decided to return to college. His mother packed a tin of *ghee* for him, since he was so thin. The poor thing thought that if he ate a tablespoonful with every meal, he'd fatten up. But our man sold the tin of *ghee* within two days. For a fix. It was the only thing he had to sell. The guilt he felt later was so corrosive that it just ate away at his insides. He had never been able to forget it. Never. I can see how he must have felt. I felt the same way, lying there with tubes stuck into my arm and my mother sitting next to me, her hands in her lap. It was one of those rare instances when I didn't sense the underlying current of hate between us.

But the fact was that guilt or no guilt, I didn't want to live. I felt I couldn't cope with life. There was no way I could go on living as though nothing had happened. I didn't want to, even if I could. I felt cheated and angry that I was still alive. Cheated, angry, heart-broken, alone and guilty.

I insisted on going back to Worli and I insisted that my parents leave me alone. I wanted to sort things out for myself. I knew I was cutting my nose to spite my face. I was scared and terribly lonely. But I was also angry with them for saving me and I wanted to make them suffer. Alone in my flat, I found that I was horrible company. My thoughts were like demons. They tormented me. Frightened, my mind was like a caged animal. After about half an hour, I grabbed my bag and left the flat, not even bothering to switch off the fan. I couldn't bear me anymore.

~

I went to see Clara, another friend of mine. She lived in a quaint old bungalow, in the Fort area, near *Kala Ghoda*. It was the sort of house one can only find in crowded, bustling Bombay. Ugly multi-storey buildings with unpainted facades and old dilapidated structures with beautiful balconies crowded and jostled around it. Even over it. Or at least that's the feeling one got because it was so cramped. It had no front or back garden because the builders had bought all the surrounding land in the early seventies. That's why it had that claustrophobic air. But inside, it was a cozy place, with teak doors and windows, black wood armchairs and oval-shaped family portraits on the walls. The house had a fine name, redolent of the Raj, in tune with the rest of the ambience — Pettigrew Bungalow. I feel somewhat ridiculous each time I take that name because Pettigrew Bungalow and *Kala Ghoda* don't really jell. But then again, *Kala Ghoda* too is actually a relic of the Raj, isn't it? It's the local name given to the statue of Edward VII seated on a horse, that used to stand at Apollo Gate. So now I'm confused — do *Kala Ghoda* and Pettigrew Bungalow jell or not? Never mind!

Clara's family has lived there for four generations. They were English. Three sisters had bought the bungalow in the early twenties. They used to run a school there, called the Private European School. Actually, they had changed the name of the house to something else — Bluedale or something. But nobody ever called it that except the three sisters. And even they had to mention "Pettigrew Bungalow" in parenthesis.

Only one of them could find a bachelor Englishman at the time when most of them were returning home, and she had married him. The others preferred spinsterhood to marrying a non-Englishman. Clara's grandmother was the married sister's daughter. I don't know whom she married. She must have managed to hunt down an Englishman too since it was only her son, Clara's father, who had spoiled everything by marrying a Parsi.

The three sisters were absolutely horrified — despite the heirloom Limoges tea-service and antique French clocks she brought with her as part of her dowry; things they themselves could not afford. The eldest sister was ninety-six at that time and the youngest was ninety-one. They didn't know what to do or say. So they just lay down and died. All within the same year. One by one. Clara says their only consolation was that her mother had been Parsi and not an *Indian* Indian. I wondered about that. The Parsis have been in India for, I don't know — a thousand years? How was it that people still think of them as *different*?

The only Christian thing that Clara does fairly regularly is to lay flowers at the sisters' graves. I went with her to the cemetery once. Jemima, Matilda and Deborah Atkinson — those were their names. The other members of Clara's family are buried there too but they weren't half as interesting as these three. We, Clara and I, learnt how to bake by following the instructions in Deborah's recipe book. Thanks to her, I bake excellent seed cake. Only, we Indians don't seem to appreciate it!

~

*C*lara had been living alone for about eight months, since her mother died. She and I were good friends but I had always stayed away from her friends and never joined them in any of their parties. Clara's descriptions of their parties always left me speechless and slightly scandalized. Sometimes I'd even blush, much to her raucous amusement. We had certain things, like cooking, that we did together but what we really did was talk. We could tell each other everything under the sun, knowing that the other would understand.

Clara was getting ready to go out when I reached her place. I sat on her bed, drinking the stiff whisky I had poured for myself and restlessly watched her as she did her eyes. I didn't want her to go but I couldn't ask her to stay. After she finished, she took one long, hard look at me and asked me to come along.

We drove down to Cuffe Parade in Clara's car. I was dressed in borrowed plumes and was already quite drunk with the whisky. Behram's flat was huge — overlooking the sea — with a great view of Bombay on the other side. The party was already in full swing by the time we reached there. Behram was a good host and good-looking too, in a slick sort of way. I think I must have drunk a whole bottle of whisky that night. After a while, I lost track of everything. I danced a lot, stopping only when the exercise sobered me down. But I stopped only to take another drink. I didn't know whom I was dancing with and I didn't care. I found everything hilarious, as though I was looking and hearing and talking from a great distance.

It was 3 a.m. by the time we drove back. I decided to stay the night at Clara's place rather than go back to that horrible flat. The thought of trying to sleep scared me. Something inside whimpered at the thought of again lying awake, with nothing but my thoughts for company.

~

*A*nd thus began what I can only call the most unfortunate phase of my life.I don't think I was sober for a single moment in the next four months. I had to have a drink even before I brushed my teeth. I smoked constantly and didn't dare go to bed without smoking a joint — it started with one and soon became too many to count. *Ganja* made me fall asleep and didn't give me horrible dreams. It also made me look like a fright. A hag. But what the heck. Who cared!

Behram became a constant visitor to my flat. Initially he would come alone. Then he started bringing a couple of friends with him. I screwed them all. At times, we had threesomes. Sometimes four of us together on the bed. After a night like that, I'd wake up the next day and throw up over and over again till there was nothing left inside. Even then, sometimes the retching wouldn't stop.

I don't know why I had that compulsive craving for sex. I hated every minute of it and I loathed myself the next morning. But I couldn't stop. I wanted to abuse my body — mutilate it. Make it like my mind. Fucked up. I think Vivek's uncalled-for and hurtful charge of 'multiple partners' also had a lot to do with it. I remember one ghastly night at Behram's place. The whole room was thick with *ganja* and cigarette smoke. There were four of us in the room, fucking on the carpet. I was drunk to the gills and had been feeling nauseous all evening. Suddenly I threw up all over the sofa, with everybody watching. And I didn't care one bit. Not one bit. I still grimace when I think of that night. I never consciously think about it but sometimes it comes back unbidden and I try to zap it away. But nobody's found a way to do that yet. So it lies there, adding to my pile of debris. Whether I talk about it or not, its there. I used to wish that it had never happened but I don't anymore. As a friend of mine once told me, once the egg is boiled there is no point in keeping it back under the hen.

I don't know how long this would have continued. Maybe I'd have eventually snapped out of it. Maybe I wouldn't have. It's hard to say because Destiny decided to take the matter into its hands. One night I was with Behram and three other men. I was stoned out of my mind. We were driving to some place — I don't think I even knew where. It had rained all afternoon and the streets were wet. Behram believed in driving dangerously. At some point, the van skidded; and Behram panicked, slamming on the brakes.

Before we knew what was happening, the van had turned over and over and over. The force threw open my door and I was flung out of the car, with my handbag and all. Wounded and bruised, but not seriously hurt, I landed near a *gully* that had a taxi stand not far from the car.

I lay there stunned and frightened, a sharp pain rising up my back, which had had scraped the road. I heard people crowding around me and then trying to help me up. From the *gully*, I watched as if there was tableau being enacted on the main road. There was a lot of noise — horns were blaring and people were yelling. They were all running towards the car. The harsh yellow streetlights made the entire scene look weird. At that moment — that precise moment — as I watched them lift the car, I realised I couldn't go on this way. It was as simple as that. One minute I was self-destructive and the next minute I wasn't.

~

I turned to the man holding me up by the elbow. He turned out to be a hard-boiled Mumbai taxi-driver. I said 'Taxi, Juhu. *Jaldi.*' He didn't dilly-dally. Five minutes after the accident, I was already out of there and on my way to Juhu. It was only four weeks later that I found out that Behram, poor chap, had died in the accident.

We drove in silence for some time. My heart was hammering in my chest and in my head and everywhere. I could hear nothing but the pounding. When we were nearing Juhu, I realized I couldn't go to my parents in that state. I was a wreck, and all skin and bone. I remembered the feeble tone in my father's voice as he spoke to the nurse, after that valium business. He was old. Sixty five. No, I couldn't go there looking like that. I leaned forward and asked the driver to take me to Worli, instead. He didn't bat an eye-lid. Just drove me back all the way to Worli.

Back in the flat that I had started to dread and despise, I forced myself into a sort of routine. I promised myself I'd make an effort just for a week. Seven days. It was perhaps the longest week of my life. I didn't drink, no matter how badly I wanted to. And I didn't smoke. It was tough — especially not smoking. I had been a heavy smoker for nearly ten years and over the last four months, I had been chain-smoking.

It wasn't that I was suddenly ashamed of myself and wanted to reform and become a "nice girl" or anything like that. And I wasn't making any promises to myself or to anybody. Nor was I out to prove that I was a victim of my circumstances. It wasn't about that at all. I didn't condemn Behram for his lifestyle. I believe that people have the right to choose and to choose again, if it no longer suits them. For me, these are not the things that matter. I believe that our Higher Selves are not going to refuse to meet us just because we smoked, drank, slept with more than one man and preferred fried beef to *dal*. In my opinion, it's okay if one is acting in a state of awareness — out of choice. And that's the reason I decided to stop everything. I hadn't been acting out choice. Other emotions had pushed me. I had become reactive. And I didn't want to be like that. I hope you understand. I mean, too bad if you don't but it would be nice if you did.

~

I forced myself to cook and eat thrice a day. I'd wake up early and walk for three hours. After breakfast, I made it a point to bathe — a thing I had stopped doing regularly. The flat was a mess — grimy and dirty; with soiled clothes in the bathroom lying in a heap that rose right up to my chest. Empty bottles were strewn everywhere and unwashed dishes lay piled near the kitchen sink. There was a stale sour smell in the flat. Like vomit. I spent afternoons cleaning up. Cleaning and airing out each cupboard and each room meticulously. At four, I'd go for another walk. Four hours this time. At eight thirty, I bathed and ate. I was in bed by nine fifteen — exhausted, but still wide-awake.

~

*O*n the eighth day, at 6 a.m., I locked the flat and took a taxi to Juhu. I haven't seen that flat ever since.

Seven

*N*othing has changed in my parents' house for years and years. The furniture is the same, the upholstery is the same, the curtains are the same — the plates, the bed-sheets, the pressure cooker — everything!

Every morning, my father sits in the same armchair and reads *The Hindu*, sipping tea from the same light-brown Hitkari coffee-mug. Only three mugs of the set have survived. By seven thirty, my mother's bath and prayer is over. The cassette player is switched on and P.Leela's *Narayaneeyam* fills the house.

Yogeendranaam
Twadamne
shwatigasumadhuram
muktibhaajaam

nivaso-ooo-OOO
Bhaktanaam,
kaamvarsha
dhwitarukhisalayammmm...

At nine, Indu *bai*, the maid, arrives. She washes and hangs the clothes out to dry in the back verandah. I can recognize my mother's petticoats anywhere — even in a *dhobi ghat*. They are the most frayed and faded of the lot. When she buys new ones, she still doesn't throw away the old ones. Those are apparently more than enough to wear at home. At eleven, my father sleeps, my mother cooks and the whole house is silent, except for the tinkling of the wind chime hanging in the sitting room. At five, my mother washes her face and applies *Oil of Olay*. She combs her hair, changes her sari and sticks a fresh *bindi* on her forehead. Both of them then go for a walk, carrying a *sanjee* for vegetables, which they will buy from the same vegetable vendor on their way back each day. At six thirty, she lights the lamp. By eight thirty, dinner is over and the T.V is switched on. My father dozes with his spectacles stuck on his forehead and my mother watches her current favorite. In those days — 1984 — I remember it was *Yeh jo hai Zindagi*. By ten they're in bed.

It's been like this ever since I can remember. Even before my father retired from his office things had not been very different. The same routine. The same peace. The same hush. Marred only by my rows with my mother. Returning home was like slipping back into a snug, secure cocoon. I reverted to my old life as if the intervening nine years had never happened. I helped in the kitchen, watered the plants in the balcony, dusted the house, polished the brass, set the table, cleared the table. I sat in the sun and oiled my hair. I made face packs with *Guruvayoor chandanam* and turmeric and applied it on my face — all the things I used to do before I left home. Everything was the same and yet everything was different.

It was a time of healing. A time of rest. Tara would drive down every Saturday, all the way from Worli to see me. We'd go for a movie or we'd sit in the balcony and watch the rain. After the first couple of visits, she stopped being a reminder of the days when I had worked for The Economic Times. She stopped being a reminder of Vivek. I learnt to relax and looked forward to Saturdays after that. She was such fun to be with! And I longed to laugh and be happy. I didn't know then that happiness wasn't an end in itself. It was a by-product — like molasses.

Clara never came to visit me. My mother didn't like her and I think she sensed that. But she phoned once in a while. I tried to call too but she was never in whenever I tried. So after a while I stopped trying. In any case, I didn't really feel like talking to anybody. I felt physically sick. I had no appetite. My mouth tasted funny. My head constantly ached and worst of all, I just couldn't sleep. That made me feel tired and listless.

I spent most mornings in the front verandah, propped up among cushions, on Becky's sofa. Becky was my dog and my best friend. She died four years ago. We were a team. She had been my companion, sitting up with me through those long nights while I studied for my exams. I had seen her through two pregnancies, countless ingrown toenails, an ear infection, an eye infection, a skin infection and tapeworms. But I wasn't there for her when she died. I had been too busy with Vivek. Things in the house that were in some way connected with her were still referred to as hers, though. Becky's sofa. Becky's window. Becky's corner.

Becky's sofa was placed on one side of the verandah and it had the best view of the street below. I sat there, watching the world go by; trying to make sense of what was happening to me and failing miserably. That restless, frantic feeling had subsided significantly but I didn't feel up to looking for another job and getting on with my life. I knew deep down that I couldn't stay with my parents forever and that I would have to move out again. But the thought of going back to Worli depressed me. I didn't see any point in finding another job and getting back to a lifestyle very similar to the one I had before — just that this time there would be no more Vivek. It would be the same lonely evenings. The same solitary meals. The same meaningless socializing and chatter to drown the silence. I didn't want to live like that anymore. Yet the idea of living with my parents did not appeal to me either.

My relationship with my mother was too painful — too volatile. It wasn't that I didn't love her. Quite the reverse, actually. I loved her too much. So much that I couldn't accept the feeling of being pushed away, as though I *revolted* her in someway. It's all very complex and if you haven't understood yet, you probably never

86

will. The other reason for my moving out nine years ago, was that I wanted my own space. And I didn't want to have to fight tooth and nail for it. I didn't want to accept a way of life — a way of thinking — that had been handed down. I couldn't not question anything. I couldn't keep quiet and tow the line. I didn't want to belong to the society for fear of sticking out. I wanted to belong because I understood. But I didn't understand. I *couldn't*. I couldn't understand our Gods, our prayers, the way we herded together like bison.

And so I left home when I was twenty — in spite of having loved it. It's something like the elephants in Guruvayoor. They were loved and worshipped. They carried the Lord on their backs every evening. But at the same time, they were in shackles — chained for life. I didn't want any chains — especially chains that I didn't understand.

I was searching for something more permanent — something that would never leave me, something that I could understand. I didn't know what I was looking for but I knew it was there somewhere — waiting for me, calling out to me. I just had to find it. And I couldn't give up until I had.

~

*S*o I sat on Becky's sofa, making puny attempts to figure things out; jumping from one alternative to another, vacillating to-and-fro; unable to think clearly or to sense the larger picture. I was drifting aimlessly — with no direction — without a reason for being.

Marriage — the mere thought of it — irritated me. It had always irritated me. Even when I was "eligible". I couldn't imagine adjusting, compromising, being tolerant and suppressed all my life — just to keep the marriage going. Everybody around me seemed to be mismatched. But they continued like bullocks hitched to a water-wheel. Never questioning or looking around themselves. Never looking up at the world and the stars. Not even looking at each other. The thought of such a life repelled me. I was better alone and of that I was sure. I couldn't marry only because I was lonely. Suppose I married and ended up twice as lonely as before? That would be terrible.

And now, after being Vivek's part-time wife for so many years, it was unthinkable. I had shaped my life to fit his. I had lead a double life. Half of me was single and independent and the other half was married, with responsibilities. When he didn't have time for me, I wore the "single" hat and when he came home, I wore the "married" hat. For eight years, I lived like that. Not one, or two, but eight — unbelievable! I can't believe I did that.

Right at the beginning, we had put his wife on a pedestal, though we never actually spoke of her. I became extra-sensitive and developed finely-tuned antennae, to detect even the slightest change in his mood. I learnt when to shut up and when to talk, what to say and how to say it. I programmed myself. It was never spontaneous and so it was never the truth. I was an actress. Like Rekha.

Changing clothes and masks to suit the script, the situation, the song — it was all make believe.

But at the same time, my feelings were not make-believe. In my mind and in my heart, I was married to him. He was the centre of my world. Now, to talk of accommodating another man ... to think of living with him, being with him, sharing a life with him, sleeping with him — it was unthinkable.

~

*S*o, if I wasn't going to try and get married and I wasn't going back to Worli and I wasn't going to live with my parents, what in heaven's name was I going to do? It was sometime then that the idea of running away to Alanghat first took root. Alanghat had always been like a grandmother I had never seen. I had heard stories about her from my mother and those stories formed an intrinsic part of my childhood. I would listen with rapt attention, never wanting the stories to end. *Then what happened?*

The more I thought about Alanghat, the more I wanted to go there. Initially, I thought I'd go for a holiday. After all, Alanghat was my ancestral house and I belonged there. But the desire to break free from Bombay was so strong that I began to think of moving there for good. I wanted to amputate a part of my life as though it were a putrid gangrene-infected piece of flesh and start afresh. A new beginning.

At that time, my father had been contemplating selling the Worli flat. He didn't want to rent it out again and he knew me well enough to know that I would never go there again. That was the funny thing about my father. I never explicitly told him anything about my life, yet he seemed to know just how bad a state I was in. He never overtly interfered with my life, never issued any ultimatums. Never pulled rank. He just stood by and watched — knowing I would reject all advice; waiting for me to ask but realizing I never will.

I had a lot of respect for him, and deep down I wanted him to be proud of me. But I didn't trust him at all. I didn't trust him because he always supported my mother during our rows. It was a strange, complex relationship that the three of us shared. A sort of now-you-see-it-now-you-don't one.

Anyway, he was going to sell the place and spend a portion of the money in restoring Alanghat. That was when I told him I would like to go there. He agreed on the condition that I go there only to restore the place. After six months, I could decide whether I wanted to live there permanently or return to Bombay. I agreed, though I knew I would never change my mind and that I would never come back.

Eight

Thiruvonam

*A*t the end of *Karkitakam*, the monsoon showed its more benevolent side. It still rained but we had long spells of intermittent sunshine. I decided to start work on the house in late August, soon after Onam. The new month, *Chingam*, had brought with it an abundant harvest and the smell of new rice greeted me wherever I went. Little girls ran about in bright new *pavadais* - long skirts - and blouses, with *kodakadakans* - dangling gold earrings - in their ears, flowers in their hair and bells around their ankles. Their laughter filled the air as they ran around, playing like butterflies in the sunshine. It was a happy time.

Alanghat became the hub of activity with workers swarming all over the place. They all looked the same. They would arrive together at about nine o' clock every morning, wearing white shirts and *mundus*, carrying a small bag in their hands, in which they carried their tools, their lunch and their work clothes. They would change into their work clothes, hanging their clean white ones neatly on a nail or folded over a railing. At the end of the working day, at 5:30 sharp, they would put down their tools, change and leave. Not once did any of them come in early or stay back after the others had left for the day. That was the diktat of the trade union.

Their work clothes were *banians* and loud-printed *lungis*. One of them even had a dark green one with huge pink roses. Underneath their *lungis*, they wore striped drawers, in the pocket of which was a pack of *beedis*. The men were all the colour of *unniappams*, a dark brown sweet, which is fried just a little too long. All of them had oily hair and scrawny legs. Some of them had Reynolds pens stuck behind their right ears and some of them had Natraj pencils. No other brand except Reynolds and Natraj.

The master craftsman was a taciturn fellow by the name of Ramachandran, pronounced *Ramaindran*. He answered all my questions with either a grunt or monosyllabic words. If he could pretend he hadn't heard, it was what he most preferred. He made me feel like I was a nuisance, always getting in the way.

However, after I realized they were good at their job, I stopped poking my nose into everything they did, counting every bag of cement they opened and every plank of wood they used. For a long time I had the feeling that one of them would try to steal the *aat-katal*, the swing bed that I had seen hanging in one of the rooms when I first came to Alanghat — the huge thing, which probably weighed a ton! So, I would walk in every fifteen minutes and casually check if it was still hanging there or not. The fact that it had hung there for twenty-five years, almost completely open to theft had slipped my mind.

~

*L*ike every town or village situated close to a river, Kunnathur also had a Brick and Tile factory. It was The Standard Brick and Tile Factory, Kunnathur. The current owners were Christians but at one time, it had belonged to the Alanghat House. That was years ago — fifty, at least. In fact, one could see the huge brick chimney of the factory if one stood at the steps leading to the river, behind Alanghat. I had visited the factory and placed an order for tiles and bricks much before work on the house actually began. I had to open the huge front-gate of Alanghat to let in the trucks, carrying the brick and tiles. That was the first time those gates had been opened in a long, long time. I had felt strange — as if I were opening the gates of a fort or something!

~

*O*nce my mind was at rest about their capability and integrity and I no longer felt the need to hover around them, I contented myself with a visit in the morning, one in the afternoon and one before they wound-up for the day. Sometimes I made "surprise checks", priding myself on my shrewdness and ability to judge character — especially the character of the working class — and to subtly let them know that their tricks would not work with me. But strangely enough, not once did I surprise them. If they were working, they continued to do so, ignoring me completely. And if they were taking a *beedi* break, they continued to do so, ignoring me completely. As usual.

Being constantly ignored was quite a blow to my ego and once I acknowledged that, my hypocrisy came as quite a revelation. It was all very fine to play the good-humored, young aristocrat when everyone like Binkity's wife, for instance, was kow-towing. Reveling in that role, I could brush aside the homage as out-dated, believing myself to be as a breath of fresh air in the stifling social environs of Kunnathur. It was okay when I was being given my due place at the top of the heap. But these workers were not doing that. They were ignoring me and at that time, I had felt insulted. I mean, didn't they know who I was!

But as they didn't seem to want me around — to hover and supervise, astound them with the way I solved all their problems, using my brilliant common sense — I found myself at a loose end. I realised I had nothing to do. So I went back to driving around in my Trax, looking at all the houses and trying to find one that resembled Alanghat. Alanghat was grand — an architectural and artistic masterpiece. Ramaindran had told me that she had been modified a few times. Perhaps that is why she seemed unique, and although there were some traditional Nair houses nearby, none of them was quite in the same class as Alanghat. She was matchless.

~

*T*he fields on either side of the roads were a golden brown now. The rain and the sun had miraculously changed green to gold. One afternoon is particularly engraved in my memory. Even after all these years, I can still remember the feel of the soft breeze on my face and the clean, fresh smell everywhere. I was driving down an open road, listening to music. And on both sides of the road, women harvesting paddy.

A new song began to play. A beautiful song about barley fields. The words, softly sung, filled the Trax and flowed out into the open air, filling the entire Universe.

You'll remember me
when the west wind moves
upon the fields of barley.
You'll forget the sun
in it's jealous sky
as we walk in fields of gold.

I began sweating and my mouth dried up. I reached down and turned off the stereo but the song just wouldn't end. It went on in my head, as though the singer was sitting inside.

In his arms she fell
as her hair came down
among the fields of gold.

By now I was driving like crazy, hurling down the narrow road as if there were demons chasing me. Children hopped off the road and stared wide-eyed at me but I was past caring. I didn't know what was happening to me except that some unknown power was forcing me to remember — to remember each moment I had spent with Vivek — and the terrible thing was that I did remember every moment. I hadn't forgotten even after all this time, despite everything that had happened. My body still remembered and reacted, as though shaken awake after a long slumber.

Feel her body rise
as you kiss her mouth
among the fields of gold.

I was trembling by the time I parked the Trax under the *peepul* tree in Nandu's house. Even today I have no recollection of how I reached there. All I remember is that mad dash down the road and then parking the Trax. I sat with my head down on the wheel for a brief moment and I think I fell asleep, though I'm not sure that I did. I opened my eyes only when I heard the sound of my door opening. A tall, thin, elderly man was standing there looking very worried. His white shirt and *mundu* were so white that I was blinded for a second. His hair was white too and so was his beard. My first impression of Solomon was a whole lot of white.

His face eased into a stiff smile when he realized I hadn't passed out, and he introduced himself. We walked in silence towards the house. I got the odd impression that he was nervous. And also reserved. He didn't say anything for a long time. Just sat there, in the front porch, and looked at me while I talked to Shailaja and joked with Amit and Sumit. But there was something funny about that look. He seemed to be studying me intently. There was also something incredulous about it, as if he couldn't believe his eyes.

He must have been about sixty at that time but he seemed much older. The skin on his face was wrinkled and his fingers were bony. It was his eyes that caught my attention from the start. They were a clear brown — the colour of jaggery. When they lit up, I knew he was happy or amused about something. But usually, they were sad. One got the feeling that his had not been an easy life. There was nothing else in his manner that gave one that impression, except his eyes. And with time, I learnt to read those eyes so well that one glance was enough to tell me all. There was no other way of knowing what was going on in his mind because he never spoke about himself at all. Not even casual things like 'I've eaten too much!'

Actually, he almost never said anything about anything. But on those rare occasions, when he did say something that was not an

97

answer to a question, it was always in a low hoarse whisper. There had to be pin-drop silence in the room if one wanted to hear what he was saying.

However, he made up for his silence by smiling a lot. He had a slow way of smiling. It started as a twinkle in his eyes and then slowly made its way to the rest of his face, transforming it completely.

Solomon and Parameshwaran had been school friends and Nandu had known Solomon all his life. Remember I once told you that he and Shailaja made a trip to Manuthy to visit him and wife, Saramma every Saturday. It became evident to me over lunch why Shailaja and Nandu thought the world of him. There was a luminous quality about him. He seemed so … light and clean. It is hard for me to describe that special something that set him apart. He was like an angel. Yes, I felt I was in the presence of an angel. That's exactly how I felt.

I was very uncomfortable that entire afternoon. I had liked Solomon immensely right from the start but I could sense that he had not made up his mind about whether to like me or not. There was a certain aloofness about him that I couldn't understand. He was comfortable and loving with Nandu and Shailaja and the kids, answering with ease their questions about why Saramma hadn't come; not at all irritated when all four of them asked the same question separately, at different times.

But with me he was cautious. At the same time, he was not indifferent. He hardly ever spoke, preferring to listen to all the chatter around him, with a small, amused smile on his face. He listened with great attention to anything I had to say, even if it was something quite stupid. Whenever I offered him a fruit or a *pappadum*, he took it whether he wanted it or not.

By the end of the visit that lasted till tea, his manner towards me relaxed and I knew I had passed the test — whatever it was. And I was thankful.

~

Solomon and I never *got to know* each other, you know. There was no gestation period. No cooking time. One day we were strangers and the next day, I had known him forever. I slipped into the habit of driving to Manuthy whenever I had some free time on my hands. I was always welcome. And I always stayed for lunch. Saramma was a wonderful cook and I spent hours with her in the kitchen, trying to figure out *Nasraaneal inte veppe*, the Christian style of cooking. Wonderful stuff! They treated me like a child, spoiling me rotten; and I enjoyed every moment of it.

Solomon spoke excellent English, which was a relief because I was getting tired of thinking in English, translating it into Malayalam and then talking. He spoke wonderful Malayalam too and I saw him trying to hide a smile more than once at my terrible pronunciation and lousy vocabulary. At the same time, he seemed to sense that I was not happy and was sympathetic about it. Never curious or probing. Just taking my questions at face value and answering them to the best of his ability. And I had a lot of questions to ask! All kinds of questions — about things like happiness and sorrow, and other things too. The Bible, the Middle East — Antioch and Syria and Israel. The Christians in Kerala. We talked a lot about the Nairs too, I remember — Oh we talked about all kinds of things! One question would lead to another and we would spend hours sitting in the porch, while outside the rain poured in buckets, wetting the steps and drenching the *techi* near the gate which grew in clumps as big as my face. If we reached an unsavory part or an unpleasant truth, Saramma would call out from inside, '*ad paranj kodkaan vella aavishyam indo! Che!*' Is there any need to tell her all that? *Che!*

~

*L*ooking back, I think the day Solomon came for lunch to Nandu's place marked the beginning of the rest of my life. My past slowly ceased to be a millstone round my neck and I began to realise, though dimly, that I still had a future. A blank canvas waiting for the brush strokes. All I had to do was to choose the colours. I felt wise and ageless when I realised that future but it was Solomon who actually carried the realisation to its logical conclusion. I had left it half way — he gave me the vital clue, the breakthrough I needed to complete the puzzle. He told me that all I really had was *now* and that I couldn't *plan* my future because I had no claim on it. I could anticipate it to a point. I could hope. I could pray. But that was all. On the other hand, my past was dead. I could do nothing to either change it or to bring it back.

Now was all I had. And my *now* doesn't take very long to become my yesterday and my tomorrow becomes my *now* just as quickly and imperceptibly. Such a simple truth! But one must realise it for otherwise, all simple truths are complex mysteries.

The same day — the fifth day of the *Makam njaatuvela* — is also important to me for another reason. Solomon. Solomon was as much as angel to me as Gabriel was to the shepherds. In terms of lifetimes, I spent very little time with him. Yet, in that brief period we forged a relationship so profound and powerful that it remains a part of me even today. And will be forever.

Nine

*S*lowly Alanghat lost that neglected, forlorn look. The tiles on the roof were changed, the walls were replastered and painted and the pillars and other woodwork treated and varnished. The grounds were swept and cleared. As the house began to take on a different look, I began to spend more and more time there, going back to Nandu's only late in the evening.

Alanghat took her time showing me her secrets, this old, old mother of mine. But when she finally did, she held nothing back. She was huge; two stories high, with rooms within rooms and small staircases that suddenly cropped out of nowhere. It was deep in the interior of the second floor, an area which had been locked and double locked — and then locked all over again (this had to be the work of an old man; old men are the most suspicious creatures in the world and they don't trust anybody) — that I found her treasures.

I spent that entire day in those rooms. With the windows open, there was just enough light to make things visible. It had rained that morning and the raindrops still dripped from the tiles, splattering into the puddle below. In one corner of the first room, there was a pile of swords, shields, spears and daggers — all blunt and rusted with age and disuse. At one time, the Nairs were supposed to have been warriors. In fact, they would have strutted about the place with their weapons — usually swords and shields though some of them even owned guns. But that was in the past. Most Nair militias were disbanded in the eighteenth and early nineteenth centuries, except for the armies of the Travancore and Cochin Rajas. After this, the Nairs grew effeminate and ineffectual, preferring a quiet swing in the porch to the violence of war.

The room also had kitchenware that none of the members of the family had cared to take with them. There were brass coffee filters of different sizes, *thalis*, *lota*-shaped tumblers, *kindies* to pour water from, spittoons, huge *varpadam* bowls for cooking (each bowl looked like a baby's bath-tub). *Varpadam* is an alloy of copper and tin that was used in Kerala back in the old days to fashion beautifully shaped bowls. Later, stainless-steel took over. There were *urlis* (flat, wide vats used for making *payasam*) and *varppus* made of *varpadam*. Behind the door on either side, brass and copper *kodams* used to store water were piled one on top of the other until they touched the ceiling. *Bharanies* — there were many *bharanies* and lots of stone and mud pots used for cooking.

Then there were the odd china bowls that did not belong to a set. A stray silver tray or spoon, chipped figurines, a lady holding an umbrella — her face missing. There were dolls too — old-fashioned porcelain *bommas* — little girls' dolls — with bonnets and aprons. And there were toy animals — sheep, cows, elephants and lots of dogs.

~

I wandered into another world that day. Another era. This was Alanghat in the year 1885, at the zenith of her power. The front courtyard would have been neatly manicured then, with lots of flowers — roses, hibiscus, lilies, jasmines, *champak* and *techi*. Further away, the garden lands would have been thick and wooded with mango, coconut, pepper, jackfruit, rosewood, teak and sandalwood. Creepers would have covered the porch — orange blossoms hanging like bells and nodding in the soft morning breeze; and outside, a horse-carriage would have waited.

There would have been a stream of visitors welcomed by the *gomastha* who would have led them in to meet the *karnavan*. The *karnavan*, dressed in off-white and gold and just about to leave for Trichur, would have sat chewing tobacco on the silk-upholstered, rosewood settee designed like a swing. As soon as he had dealt with the last visitor, he would have walked to the carriage and sat erect on the burgundy velvet seat; his back upright and his cane resting at his side. His *gomastha* would have huddled into an inconspicuous bundle next to him. The coachman would close the carriage door and drawn by two lively black horses, the wheels would clatter beneath an arbor of jasmine, and down the long driveway lined with lilies and hibiscus and pink roses, beyond which, in the dense grove of — I looked out of the window — yes, in the dense grove of jackfruit trees, a herd of deer lived. The mango tree must have been there at that time too. Young. Perhaps a sapling. The massive gates would open and the *karnavan* of Alanghat would have set out on his way to Trichur, acknowledging nobody on the road other than his social equals, of which there were very few in Kunnathur and the surroundings villages. So on most days, he would have acknowledged no one, while the commoners on the street would have bowed humbly.

In those days, Kerala had a land system that was quite — well, *weird*. Solomon had told me the story during one of our marathon sessions on the steps of his porch. According to him, the highest in the pecking order were the *jenmies*. Most *jenmies* in the other parts of Kerala were *Nambutiris*, the Brahmins. Since not many of them settled down in this part of Malabar, we became paramount. Had there been a *Nambutiri* family in our area, Alanghat's story would have taken an altogether different turn.

The land owned by *Nambutiri jenmies* was transferred on *kanam* tenure to the Nairs. As the Nairs were placed pretty high up in the caste hierarchy, they too decided that hard labour was not for them and their holdings were passed on to the *kuzhikanakaran* — a man who held a tenure on the land and enjoyed its yield for a specific period. Below him was the actual cultivator — the *verumpattakaran*, who belonged to the lower castes.

A characteristic feature of this system of caste and land-holding of pre-British Malabar, was "joint-partnership". The principal land-holders — the *jenmi,* the *kanakaran* and the *verumpattakaran* — were part-proprietors. As custom dictated, each of them were entitled to one-third or an equal share of the net produce of the land. The net produce was the yield left after the other customary claimants — the village carpenter, the goldsmith and the labourers were given their share.

The rot set in when the British took over Malabar in the early eighteenth century. They conferred absolute ownership rights on the *jenmies*, without caring to understand the complex nuances of the traditional system. Or perhaps they understood it only too well but went ahead anyway, to get the *jenmies* on their side. Once the *jenmi* was no longer dependent on the other claimants for security or for anything else, he began to impose harsher terms on the *kanakaran*, who passed it on down the pecking order. This was the root of the unjust and oppressive land system that held the tenants and cultivators in its thrall for more than a hundred years. It was in 1920 that the Kanam Tenants Agitation began, leading to the formation of the Malabar Kudian (tenant) Sangham and the passing of the controversial Malabar Tenancy Bill. The formation of the Karshaka Sanghams and the Verumpattom Agitation by the 1930s laid the foundation for the Communist movement and even today, Malabar remains the bastion of the Communist party in Kerala.

A foundation was also laid for what is perhaps the most radical of all social reforms through legislation in the world. This was the Kerala Land Reforms (Amendment) Act of 1969. The main demand on its agenda was the abolition of the feudal system to give the land to the tiller. All at once, it destroyed forever the power of the Nair *jenmies* and the position of the *Nambutiris*, pushing them into a pit of oblivion from which they haven't yet climbed out.

~

*B*ut as usual, I digress. Back in Alanghat, peace and quiet descends on the house, with the *karnavan* out of the way. The day passes slowly. Leisurely. Upstairs, in a four-poster bed, fanned by one of the maids, one of the ladies is sleeping. In the bathing tank, another lady is getting ready for her bath. Her bath will take - maybe, two hours.

First, she her body will be anointed with five kinds of oils and scrubbed gently with an aromatic mixture of herbs and sandalwood. Bathed, gleaming and fragrant, she would dress in a fresh *kasava mundu*, slip on gold bangles, chains, ear rings and nose rings. She will smear her eyes with *kohl* and then walk down at five o' clock in the evening, resplendent as the morning sun.

Smiling, she will address all her visitors by name, calling for some *payasam* or some coffee, if the visitor is important. Else, graciously accepting obeisance. Patroness of the arts, she will sit on a divan (now lying forgotten in a corner next to the four poster bed) and chew betel leaves till her lips are red and be entertained by musicians and dancers, swaying to the beat of the *mridangam* and the tinkle of bells.

Outside, in the smoke-filled kitchen, a woman is grinding coconut into a paste in the huge stone grinder. Another one is chopping vegetables for the *avial*, and yet another one is drawing water from the well. They are the lesser mortals. The cooks are superior human beings, instructing, commanding and supervising. Everything has to be right — the size of vegetables, the consistency of the coconut paste, the amount of *kayam*, asafoetida. There is a family for dinner that day. A family dinner for sixty people. All the six burners have *vengala paatrams* bubbling on them. The aroma of chicken curry fills the whole room and wafts out into the back yard where the Alanghat boys, under the expert tutelage of a master, are in the midst of their *kalaripayat* training session. The younger boys, wearing nothing but a loincloth, their bodies glistening with oil, are standing on one side, watching the older "men" practice with swords and shields; wondering when, if ever, they would reach that level. In the shade of the tamarind tree, there is a huge tusker watching the boys heft and heave, twist and thrust; swaying with interest and sometimes, amusement.

The little girls are playing with their dolls in another room. House-house. Or school-school. Or shopkeeper-shopkeeper. One of the mothers calls and they run down, their skirts fluttering bright against the heavy teak staircase, their little feet noiseless on the wood.

~

*T*hat must have been the year 1885. Now, a hundred years later...

It had started raining again, very heavily and the room had become dark. I sat there in that musty room holding the lady with the missing face, wondering where it had all gone. No servants, no preparations for a feast, no women in the bathing tank, no dancers, no mighty warriors and no children playing outside. Alanghat was in rags, like Cinderella. Her carriage had turned into a pumpkin and her horses had turned into bandicoots. Not mice but bandicoots. Big, black and hairy.

~

I got up slowly, my knees stiff after having sat cross-legged for so long. There were two more rooms left to open. One was a small cubby-hole filled with old records and *olas* that might have been the accounts of expenses incurred in the running of the estate.

The door to the next room was jammed and I had to push with all my might. The first thing I saw was the veena lying in a corner, wrapped in deep blue velvet. I stood still, unable to believe my eyes. Here, too! My veena was everywhere — omnipresent. I had literally to drag my eyes away from the veena, and only then did I realize that the small room was full of instruments. There was the veena, a harmonium, a sitar, a mridangam...even a tabla! Here in tiny Kunnathur, far away in the south, way back in the thirties or forties, somebody had learnt to play the tabla. Somebody had the yearned to do so. This person had had music in his blood. It had to be a man because not many women played the mridangam and the tabla. But who was this man? I knew only of Keshavan Nair. Was it him? Had *he* cursed me with this gift? But why me? Why hadn't I been allowed to go free?

~

I would sit on the old *aat-katal* I had asked Ramaindran to hang in the porch and listen to the mango tree singing to itself. I found myself more and more curious about what had happened here. What were the "strange happenings"? What was the "tragedy" all about?

I knew a bit. A somewhat highly edited version everybody thinks is right for children to know. There had been a fight in the family — a great family feud which had started in 1928 and which finished in 1950, the year my parents married and moved to Bombay.

Following a court decree in 1940, the property had been divided equally between Rugmani Devi, her three sisters and two brothers. Since we were Nairs, we followed the *marumakatayam,* or the matrilineal system where each family traced its ancestry to a common female ancestor. At the same time, we were not matriarchal because the head of the family was the oldest maternal uncle - the *ammaman* - and his heir was his eldest nephew, the eldest of all

111

his sisters' sons. In fact, that is broadly what *marumakatayam* means — a tradition where the *marumagan* or nephew is the heir. Because of this system, the families of Rugmani Devi and her three sisters were also entitled to one share each. That is all I knew about the Great War.

What really happened between 1940 and 1950 was a mystery. From what I could figure out, after we had lost all our land in the feud, only one person remained in Alanghat and that was my mother's mother. She lived here alone for nearly six years.

One morning, she disappeared. The maid who worked here during the day came at the usual time and found the huge front door wide open and the house empty. Nothing had been stolen, nothing had been disturbed. The only aberration was that my grandmother had vanished without trace.

The village people said that the *udianmaar* had taken her away. *Udianmaar*, as far as I knew, were strange creatures - neither man nor beast - that came from the world of spirits, and who could take on any human form they chose – people you knew, sometimes even relatives. They could assume a particular form, come to you at night, shake you awake and take you far into the fields and kill you.

the villagers were convinced that that is what had happened to my grandmother. My poor mother never spoke about it. No matter how much I badgered her, she would just keep quiet. My parents came to Alanghat, leaving me in Bombay with friends, when this happened and spent six months here searching for her. But she had disappeared without a trace. That was the last time my mother had set foot in Kunnathur.

This was all I knew. But it was no longer enough. It had never been enough but now after seeing Alanghat and living here in Kunnathur for so long, I had to know more. I had written to my mother asking her again, for the umpteenth time to tell me what had happened but her reply ignored that bit completely.

Who else could tell me? I still didn't feel comfortable asking Nandu or Shailaja though I toyed with the idea many times. Once I even made up my mind to speak to them about it but I could not. I didn't want to hear the story from them. There was only one person with whom I felt I could talk about my family — Solomon. I felt I could talk to him about anything. He had been Parameshwaran's school friend, so he must have been around when all these things happened. He would know. Something, if not everything. At least, he would know more than I did.

So I drove to Manuthy the next day, taking some of the more interesting-looking *olas* with me. Solomon was sitting in the front porch reading the newspaper. Saramma was nowhere to be seen. I sat down on the ledge and, without a second thought, asked him what I had to. No matter how hard I try, if there is something on my mind, out it comes.

The change in his expression stunned me. One minute it was affectionate, loving and amused and the next minute it was tense, serious and deeply troubled. I stared at him, surprised. I hadn't thought the subject any different from all the other things we had

113

talked about for hours and hours. Why should long-forgotten events in my family trouble him so much? But they did. He sounded hoarse and curt in his refusal to so much as mention a word about it. The way he said it hurt and I couldn't hide the feeling soon enough. I had changed from the old days that I told you about earlier. *Never let your feelings show…* . He saw the pain in my eyes but didn't say anything. There was a tension and awkwardness between us but I stayed for lunch anyway. It was what I usually did when I visited them.

~

*S*olomon stayed away for a whole week. He didn't call or stop by and that confused me even more. What was the matter with him? I found out on the eighth day at five-thirty in the morning. I was sitting in the front porch after yet another sleepless night when I saw him walk up to the house. Nandu's house doesn't have a gate or a compound wall or even a driveway leading up to it. You just turn off the road and walk or drive in the general direction of the house.

He sat down slowly on the chair opposite mine, tired after his walk from the bus-stand. He must have taken the first bus down. He was silent for some time, marshalling his thoughts. I watched him, waiting for him to say something. It had taken him all this time to decide whether he should tell me the story or not. And he had finally decided that I had the right to know. He said it was better that I heard the truth from him rather than gossip from the villagers.

He began with a question. 'Do you know that you are the spitting image of your grand uncle?'

Ten

Solomon got up from his chair and came to sit next to me on the steps leading to the porch. His eyes had the same incredulous expression that I had seen that day we first met, right here in Nandu's house. His hand lifted my chin and he turned my face towards him so that we were staring at each other. In that pearly morning light, his eyes looked specked with green and they had a curious molten quality.

'If Raman Nair had been a woman, he'd have looked like you.' Solomon was speaking to himself, his hoarse whisper somehow merging with the rustle of *peepul* leaves. I could hear him only because we were sitting so close together — so close that I could feel his breath fanning my cheek. The fingers on my chin tightened and he continued, 'The same forehead... the eyes... the expression... everything is the same. It's almost like he has come back to

Alanghat. To settle...' Solomon fell silent for so long that I thought he'd finished what he had to say. I tried to make some sense of those last words. To settle. To settle what? Down? Matters?

'Unfinished business.' Solomon spoke again, letting out a deep breath and the way he spoke caused shivers to run down my spine. He got up suddenly and started walking to the back of the house. I followed, knowing intuitively that he was going to the well, from where one could see the high undulating roof of Alanghat. He leaned against the well and stared at the roof. I stared too but I couldn't see what he was seeing, no matter how hard I tried. So I looked away and started fidgeting with the bucket and rope — drawing the bucket up and letting it fall till it hit the water in the well with a *thunk*. I did that over and over again — *thunk, thunk, thunk*. I was Raman Nair and I had come back to settle unfinished business. *Thunk*. Raman Nair was my grand uncle and I looked like him. *Thunk*. Was that so amazing? *Thunk. Thunk. Thunk. Thunk.*

Solomon whirled around and grabbed the rope from my hand. '*Shhh*!' he hissed. 'Can't you ever be still? Stop fidgeting!'

I glared back at him, 'I am Raman Nair and I've come back to settle unfinished business — what sort of a stupid story is that?' I waved my hands about as I spoke and rolled my eyes.

'You even speak like him.' Solomon was staring at me. Then he shook his head and looked away. 'No, no - you aren't Raman Nair. That's not what I mean. It's just that you look so much like him, its uncanny. You see, Raman Nair was murdered. By your

118

uncle - your mother's brother, Narayanankutty.' Solomon broke off when he noticed my expression. 'You didn't know that, did you? You didn't know that your mother had an older brother.' He smiled and stroked my hair, then took a deep breath and continued. 'Narayanankutty and Nandu's father, Parameshwaran, were very good friends. Narayanankutty — Nanu he was called — Nanu and I were friends too but we were not as close. Nobody was as fond of Nanu as Parameshwaran was. Not even Nanu himself. In Parameshwaran's eyes Nanu could do no wrong. He even tried to pass off the murder as an accident! Even though the whole world knows that Nanu waited for Raman Nair to return from the village late one evening — waited forty five minutes — and when Raman Nair had almost reached the gates of Alanghat, Nanu walked up to him and stabbed him thrice with a kitchen knife — you know that *koduvaal*, the one we use to break coconuts — stabbed him thrice in the stomach with a *koduvaal*. Raman Nair died on the spot.'

Solomon stopped and rubbed his forehead wearily. He looked down and started sweeping the loose earth about with his foot. 'Some accident!' he snorted. 'Blind old fool, that Parameshwaran!' Solomon's voice was rough with affection and exasperation. 'Of course, we wouldn't have been old then, would we? Must have been around eighteen or nineteen. But never once until he died, did Parameshwaran actually say that Nanu had killed Raman Nair. Always spoke of it as an accident. And he was there when it happened. He was on his way to Alanghat, walking just a little behind Raman Nair. All this happened *there*, you know.' Solomon broke off to point to the lane that connected Alanghat, perched as she was on top of the hill, to the rest of Kunnathur — the lane I had walked up and down a thousand times by now. I stared at it. Such an ordinary lane! 'According to Parameshwaran, if Nanu had wanted to kill Raman Nair, he would have run away after doing so. But he didn't do that. He just stood there, staring at the body, the *koduvaal* still hanging from his hand. He didn't hear Parameshwaran cry out and run towards him. He didn't hear a thing Parameshwaran was saying. He just stood there staring — breathless, as if he had run a marathon. Then he dropped the *koduvaal*, knelt down beside Raman Nayar's body and lifted his head in both his hands. He shook it as if he was trying to wake him up. When there was no response from Raman Nayar, he laid the head down again and slowly looked up. It was only then that he saw Parameshwaran.

Nanu admitted his guilt and was sent to jail. Nobody ever saw him after that. Parameshwaran says that the last he heard, Nanu had left for Dubai. Whether he returned or not, we don't know. The villagers say he died there but nobody really knows.' Solomon stopped here. I looked around me, expecting the world to have changed and wasn't at all surprised to see that it was broad daylight now. Shailaja was standing in the verandah and waving to us. 'Breakfast must be ready', I said.

We walked back to the house in silence. Throughout breakfast, Solomon was deep in thought — as if he was reliving the past. He didn't speak again until we returned to the porch and once again sat down on the steps; the same place where he had started telling me the story. I was subdued now, shocked by what I had just heard. Solomon, seeing that, smiled at me. A humourless but sympathetic smile. 'There's more — the story's not over yet.' He took my hand in his, squeezed it and again said, 'There's more.'

'Why did Nanu hate Raman Nair so much that he wanted to kill him?' Solomon turned away from me as I asked that and didn't answer immediately.

'Nanu didn't hate Raman Nair. Quite the opposite, actually. He worshipped him.' Solomon stopped again, shaking his head in despair. 'How do I explain! How do I explain what happened in that house,' he said, turning to look once again at Alanghat's roof.

'Let me start with Alanghat herself. Then maybe the rest will follow.' His voice dropped to a mere murmur. 'It was all so long ago — or wasn't it? Time's playing tricks on me.'

Eleven

*T*he Alanghat family had been *jenmies*, the absolute owners of
25,000 acres of wet and garden land. We had been as powerful as
kings for more than a century. According to the old records I found
in that cubby-hole and which I had shown Solomon, Alanghat had
owned other lands too — forest land in the hills of Vaniambadi,
Noorani, Alambalam, Thathamangalam, Nellisserri, Nelliampathi
and Vengasserri. I am not certain how much.

Although I don't know exactly how long the family had been
living in Alanghat, I do know that in 1845, we were well-
established. I know because among the old records and *olas*, I
found a *panchangam* - almanac - dated 1845. Actually, there were
fifteen of them in random order, the oldest dated 1845.

There were also some accounts in the records, of expenses
incurred in the year 1890 for various temple activities. All leading

thravaats had the *melkoyma* - the overlordship - of the temples within their region. Control over a temple didn't simply mean the exercise of influence over a community of worshippers. It also meant an access to the stocks of grain a temple commanded. Alanghat had the right of *melkoyma* over four temples. The tenants of the rice fields held by these temples paid their rent in kind and the annual demand on just one of these temples was, according to the records, 40,000 *paras* or measures. Which is a lot of rice. A lot.

Those dusty old temple records had references to *Ganapathi Homam, Thulam Vaave, Chitra Pournami, Gomapathi Puja, Makha Kazcha Adiyanthiram, Shivarathri, Sashti Sadhya, Thooku Vilakku Vazhipadu, Thiruvathira Uttu, Pindam Adiyanthiram, Navarathri, Thiruputhari Adiyanthiram, Thiruvonam, Bharani Mahatmyam, Annabhishekham, Thrikala Puja* and *Karkada Vaave*.

Along with these celebrations, which must have cost Alanghat plenty, there were also references to family celebrations. *Visu Kayneetam, Thiru Nalu, Thiru Maasam, Sanchayanom, Thirandu Kuli, Theeyatt, Narana Bali for Thirunal, Saharsa bhojanam for Thirunal, Dhanishta Santhi, Pallikeetu, Kali Arangetram, Palli Vetta, Onampudva, Grahapravesham* and *Tali Kettu Kalyanam.*

At the turn of the century, Alanghat employed at least a hundred people, so says another register. Supervisors, typists, foresters, peons, cooks, house-boys, people for measuring rice, people for collecting rent, chamber maids, gardeners, sweepers, scavengers, *mahouts*, drivers, ox-cart drivers, cowherds, cleaners, milk women, washer women, water carriers, so on and so forth. All these workers would have belonged to the lower castes and they would have lived solely on the bounty of Alanghat. Their salaries would have ranged from thirty-five rupees for the Supervisor to eight annas for the scavenger.

I found an interesting entry in the same register. According to that register, in 1902, 'Sunlight' soap had cost 5 annas, four pounds of sugar had cost 3 annas and 8 paise, one *palam* of garlic had cost 1 anna and four pounds of candles had cost 5 annas. Had the *gomastha* who entered those figures made a visit to Alanghat at the time the repair work was going on, he'd have died all over again — of shock! The basic renovation alone cost me fifty lakhs.

~

*U*nlike many Nayar (Solomon said that "Nair" was the anglicized spelling and the true blue "Nayar*s*" prefer to spell their name with a "ya".) joint families, my family was not a huge cumbersome one with many divisions and sub divisions. It was all under one head or *karnavan*. Although I have no idea when exactly the family came to be live in this house and on this land, I do know that Shankunni Nayar, along with a few relatives, broke away from the original Alanghat house which was somewhere near Alathur, and started his own branch of the family. I presume that the Raja of Kollengode gifted him this land at around the same time and that is why he left Alathur and moved to Kunnathur. However, this is a conjecture – there is no proof that this land was a gift from the king. For all you know, it's just a local legend.

~

*T*he size of each generation in Alanghat grew steadily smaller over the years. The generation preceding Rugmani Devi Amma's had only two sisters and no brothers. Of the two women, one died of smallpox soon after giving birth to a daughter. So, at the time the old *Karnavan* died, there was no one to take his place because his heir, Rugmani Devi Amma's brother was born seven years later. That is how my great-grandfather, Keshavan Nayar came to play such an important role in the history of Alanghat. He was married to Rugmani Devi, the eldest daughter of the remaining sister, when she was sixteen and he was twenty-one. Being the only male in the family, he took charge of the entire estate and continued to look after it and the family even after Rugmani Devi's two brothers were born seven years later, a year from each other. Two of Rugmani Devi's younger sisters also got married but their husbands played a secondary role, accepting Keshavan Nayar as the head of the family.

Rugmani Devi had no father. Her mother, Devaki never married. In those days, Nayars did not marry. They were free to have as many lovers as they desired, initiating what was called a *sambandham* or relationship with each of them. A woman's identity was determined not by a man but from the joint family, which carried the name of the house. She also had a share in the family property. The children of the women grew up in the *tharavaat* or family house and took on the name of the *tharavaat*. Who their father was, was irrelevant. According to some, this system had been devised to keep the family unit strong and undivided during a time when the Nayar men were warriors and had to spend long stretches away from home.

The other reason is more plausible. The *Nambutiris* had a patriarchal family structure with primogeniture as its characteristic feature. The younger sons of *Nambutiri* families could not marry and had no right to property. Since they could not marry, they formed liaisons with high-caste Nayar women. The children who were born from these unions grew up in the Nayar *tharavaat* and took its name. The father had no responsibilities.

I believe this was the real reason for the evolution of the strange Nayar custom. In Malabar, where *Nambutiris* were fewer in number than in other parts of Kerala, the women usually entered into a single *sambandham* which was very much like a marriage. The custom of having several *sambandhams* was strong in Central Kerala and Travancore, where the *Nambutiri* were higher in number. The *Kiriyath* Nayars, being the caste immediately below the *Nambutiris*, had to accomodate the *Nambutiris* in these areas.

Left to themselves, I doubt if the Nayars would have chosen a system of family life where a man had no right over his children and a woman was given sexual freedom — and not chosen it.

Such a system could only have evolved out of the selfishness of the *Nambutiri* men and the servility and the instinct for self-preservation of the Nayar*s*.

Anyway, for whatever reason, there is no mention of Rugmani Devi's father anywhere and so Solomon said we must presume that there wasn't one.

The time I am talking about here, was one of tumult and confusion for the Nayar*s*. On the one hand, younger *Nambutiri* sons had fought for - and won - the right to marry and the right to a share of the family property; finally giving *Nambutiri* women — who would otherwise have lived and died, secluded in their *illams* — a reason to live. So the *Nambutiris* no longer needed the services of Nayar women.

On the other hand, many Nayar*s* were opting for a western education, like Keshavan Nayar, who was an advocate. Increasingly uncomfortable with their family traditions, they began lobbying for the formalization of sambandhams into marriage. Also, the *Karnavans* were now tending to look after the interests of their own wives and children, rather than that of the *tharavaat*. Eventually, nearly all the younger male members of the Nayar *tharavaats* were demanding that the hitherto indivisible joint-family property be made legally divisible. Debates on these issues raged among educated Nayar*s* for thirty years and lead to the formation of the Marumakatayam Committee, the passing of the Malabar Marriage Act and the formation of the Nayar Service Society. All these advances towards radical reform in the Nayar society culminated in 1925, with the passing of the second Nayar Act (the first was in 1913) which allowed for the almost unrestricted division of the *marumakatayam* property.

~

*B*y this time, Rugmani Devi's brothers had grown up. They were educated in Madras where they failed the University exam for the Bachelor of Arts degree three and two times respectively. They were divinely handsome, suave and rotten to the core.

The quarrel between them and Keshavan Nayar — the man who had for all practical purposes been their father — began in 1928. Even though the elder one was *Karnavan,* neither of them wanted to live at Alanghat. They preferred cosmopolitan Madras. But they needed — and took — a lot of money to support their extravagant lifestyles.

Finally, after a lot of bickering and with a lot of rancor, the family went to court. The court gave its verdict in 1940, twelve years later, when the land struggle was at its zenith.

~

*T*hey had reason to be bitter — those two brothers. The reason was that Keshavan Nayar, the biggest *jenmi* in the whole district (where the entire populace comprised either tenants or debtors or both) and with the *melkoyma* or overlordship of four temples —

the very embodiment of feudalism; critical of the Congress party's inability to take a firm stand on the issue of tenant rights and disillusioned by Gandhi – became a Communist. And very vocally, at that.

He had been an active agitator in the Vaikom Temple, Satyagraha, and was one of the founder members of the Malabar Kudian Sangham, formed in 1922 in Pattambi. Throughout his life, he maintained close ties with T Rama Kurup, the first President of the *Sangham*.

He even used his ability to write in English by publishing scathing articles in the *Madras Mail* and *The Hindu*. He wrote in Malayalam too and his articles were published in the *Mathrubhumi, Kudiyan* and *Mitavadi*. It was during this period that he started the Rugmani Devi English Medium School for Girls and the Veterinary Hospital in Kunnathur. Because of his more liberal leanings, he despised the old Nayar ways and campaigned hammer and tongs for a change in the Nayar community. He was right there in the fore-front during the formation of the Nayar Service Society.

He was a very short, diminutive man who never wore a *kudumi* — the Nayar way of tying hair in a tuft in the front of the head. His attire was a funny combination of Malayali and British, considered very elegant in those days. A *mundu,* a shirt, a coat and a walking-stick. He sported a small mustache too — a cross between Charlie Chaplin and Hitler. And he had a terrible temper — attributed to the fact that he was born at ten in the morning, when the sun had already risen.

His larger-than-life personality had everybody in awe of him — even though it was they who towered over him. He was arrogant and egotistical by nature and since nobody had the courage to talk to him, let alone disagree with him, he became insensitive to the feelings of other people in his family, especially the younger generation. That was the one big flaw in his otherwise powerful personality — a flaw that blinded him to the fact that there was another young idealist in the same house, right under his very nose.

Raman Nayar was my grand uncle, Rugmani Devi's sister's son. Raman Nayar was actually *Karnavan* as he was the earlier *Karnavan's* eldest nephew. Like all the other Alanghat children, he had been sent to Madras for his college education, but unlike the others, he had been good at studies. He also had a passion for music and had opted for music as the subject for his degree.

Raman Nayar had been happy-go-lucky, handsome fellow, with twinkling eyes — always up to some wild thing or the other; and he was always laughing. At the same time he had a terrible temper too, just like Keshavan Nayar, and could flare up over any trifling thing. In 1942, he returned home after a long stint in Madras, with a Masters Degree in Music and a heart brimming with Gandhi and the Nationalist Movement, only to find that during the years of his absence, Alanghat had turned into a sort of Red Flag Hall and everybody including his mother, had become Communists. Worse, Gandhi was openly dismissed as an idle dreamer and the cause of the mess in the North.

At about the same time, Keshavan Nayar temporarily set aside Marx and Lenin and prudently bought the house and five acres of surrounding garden land from his sisters-in-law and registered it in my grandmother's name. Sharada Devi was his only child and she had been widowed young. He knew that things would turn out badly for the *jenmies* and he didn't want her to be destitute. However, he did this just before Raman Nayar — the eldest nephew and the therefore, the head of the family — returned from Madras.

Shortly after that, Rugmani Devi handed over her entire share of 25,000 acres to the tenants in a public show of support for her husband's radical, leftist beliefs. This alienated her from her sisters and Raman Nayar used the situation to his advantage. He now hated Keshavan Nayar with a vengeance; both for deriding Gandhi and for buying the house behind his back. Raman Nayar suddenly changed from being the good-humoured, endearing boy who was the darling of the family, to an angry, venomous and vindictive man whose hatred towards his uncle replaced the twinkle in his eye with a malevolent gleam.

The situation at Alanghat worsened between 1942 and 1947. Sisters fought amongst themselves. Their children fought each other. Alanghat was divided by imaginary boundaries. Each family kept a separate kitchen. Each day there was a fresh squabble. And right at the helm, there were Keshavan Nayar and Raman Nayar fighting too, over Gandhi.

In July 1947, Rugmani Devi died. Overnight, Keshavan Nayar

— already an old man — lost his seemingly indomitable spirit. He grew shriveled, wrinkled and frail, but he still fought with his nephew. A day after Gandhi's assassination, on the top of the steps that led down to the river, Raman Nayar and Keshavan Nayar had their last fight. Keshavan Nayar was coming up the steps and Raman Nayar was going down. They had a blazing row, yelling at the top of their voices, their faces red and their chests heaving. Raman Nayar gripped his uncle by the arms and shouted, *'You old dog, I'll kill you!'* giving the old man a violent push. Keshavan Nayar fell headlong down the steps — dead, even before he hit the ground.

~

*T*he story doesn't end there. Raman Nayar reported the death as an accident; and there was nobody to contest him. His own mother never said a word. Neither did his brother and sister. My grandmother, Sharada Devi had no *locus standii*, even though the house was hers. Such was the power of the men folk. The children were too young. My mother Ammu, was seventeen. Her elder brother Narayanankutty, was twenty. The police had no choice but to accept Raman Nayar's version, though the whole village was buzzing with gossip.

This was around the time the Congress party had come into power in Madras. Kerala had not yet been given statehood. The policy concerning tenancy rights, adopted by the Congress Party soon after Independence, was seen as a terrible betrayal *(by whom?)* and the Communists rose in militant revolt. Huge *Jathas* were taken out and people were shouting slogans like *Telangana Way, Our Way.* Alanghat, so long a supporter of the Communists, suddenly became a Congress supporter. Raman Nayar plunged into the political arena and supported the Congress in quelling the Communists, several of whom were known to him through Keshavan Nayar. He also began attending all the *jenmi* meetings, even organising a few of his own at Alanghat.

Now the spotlight shifts to Narayanankutty, my mother's elder brother. All his life, he had hero-worshipped Raman Nayar. He would wait for the university to close for the holidays, so Raman Nayar could return to Alanghat. That was the time he loved best. The entire house became vibrant and alive when Raman Nayar was around; there was music and the sound of laughter. And good food too, because Raman Nayar was a favourite with all his aunts. The two of them would swim in the river, play tennis, stage mock duels to entertain the family— All kinds of wonderful things would happen when Raman Nayar came home.

But now, he watched his hero change from a laughing, happy, idealistic young man to a sullen, venomous one, and he began to loathe him. On that awful day, he had stood helplessly and watched Raman Nayar *kill* the man that he, like the rest of the family, revered. That, to him, seemed like the last straw — nothing could get worse than that.

However, something worse did happen. Raman Nayar began

demolishing everything Keshavan Nayar had stood for and worked towards all his life; publicly belittling and denouncing him as an old fool, who was better dead than alive. And Narayanankutty couldn't bear that. One night, when Raman Nayar was returning from the village, Narayanankutty accosted him. Taking him by surprise, he stuck a kitchen knife - a *koduvaa* - into him. Thrice. Until he was sure Raman Nayar was well and truly dead and couldn't die anymore.

This time the police stepped in and Narayanankutty was sentenced for life. He was twenty at that time and just getting ready to leave for Madras, to join the University. He went to jail instead and nobody ever saw him again. Some say he eventually went to Dubai and became a *lakshaprabhu,* a millionaire. Who knows — perhaps he did!

Raman Nayar's mother, brother and sister left for Calcutta shortly after that. The brother, Krishnan Nayar found a good job with a newspaper there. My mother Ammu, married and moved to Bombay. The family of Rugmani Devi's youngest sister had left for Malacca in 1947. Only my grandmother stayed behind, waiting for Nanu to return. But she too disappeared six years later. No one knows where.

That is how Alanghat, queen of *tharavaats,* came to be neglected and forgotten for twenty-five years; nursing her sorrows in silence and dreaming of the days when her children had been happy and she had been young.

Twelve

I sat there in the porch long after Solomon had left, staring into the night and listening to the *peepul* tree rustling in the wind. Not really thinking about anything. Just sitting and staring. Of all the things Solomon had told me that day, only one kept whirring round and round in my head. *Did you know that you are the spitting image of your grand uncle?* No, I hadn't known. I hadn't even known that I'd *had* a grand uncle. Or even an uncle, for that matter.

It took time for Solomon's story to seep into my head. It had shaken me but it had also given me the answers to hundreds of questions, some of which I hadn't even formulated in my head. For a few days, I felt like somebody in a dream. Sort of dazed. Slowly I put together everything and wondered whether that was how my mother saw me — the *spitting image* of Raman Nayar, her uncle. The man who had murdered her grandfather, even as she watched. The man who her brother had murdered. Her only child was the *spitting image* of that man — a constant reminder. What a terrible cross to have to bear! For both of us.

Then the floodgates opened and I needed to talk to somebody. To *Solomon* — not just anybody! I reached out for him, something within me believing firmly that he would redeem me; that he would lead me out of darkness and into light. It was much later that I was able to crystallize into a definite thought what I had then known by instinct; and that is when I was able to understand the magnitude and depth of his compassion — and his goodness. But that was much, *much* later.

At the time he told me the story, he had known that I was a deeply disturbed and unhappy person. He had known that this was a story that could either restore me or destroy me, and yet he had volunteered to take on that immense responsibility. And that is why he had so painstakingly gone into the smallest of details, leaving nothing out but at the same time keeping everything within context — always giving me the right picture.

Perhaps that is what released my spirit. Else, it is possible that the story could have wrecked me even further. It is because of him that I didn't end up hating Raman Nayar, the man whose 'spitting image' I am. On the contrary, I think I seemed to understand him. If I had ended up hating him, I would have entered another emotional tunnel — a long one.

Solomon became my confidante. Sitting on the steps of his small house in Manuthy, I talked to him about my mother. He was very silent but he listened compassionately as I raked up all the grudges — some old, some new, some half-buried, some almost forgotten - a*lmost* forgotten, but still there, and still capable of hurting me.

When he had heard me out and when there was nothing left to tell, he gave me his considered opinion. He didn't think my mother hated me because I resembled Raman Nayar, though the uncanny resemblance was bound to have had a considerable effect on her. In fact, he didn't think she hated me at all. He seemed to think, from what I told him, that she just hadn't understood a child's emotional needs. Maybe she hadn't seen many children — after all, a person isn't born a good parent. One just learns as one goes along. There were parents who didn't know how to relate to their children when they were small but who could relate to them and be supportive, when they were older. It is possible that my mother was like that. In any case, he said, nobody had had the time to meet her own emotional needs when she was a child — everybody was too busy fighting. That is probably why my father supported her all the time. He realised she needed that approval. In many ways, she was as much a child as I was, and I was being a fool if I expected her to change.

As Solomon talked, I found myself sympathizing with Ammu. We were in this together. Both of us were victims. Both of us had lost the game even before we had started playing it. I had to understand my mother as a person in her own right — separate from me, an individual with needs and fears of her own. Only then could I be free — free from the feeling of always having been neglected by her.

'Not only do you have to understand', Solomon said, holding my hand in both of his, 'you have also to forgive and forget. Cast off this burden like one would cast the ashes of the dead into the sea. You'd be doing both of you a big favour. And me —', he added, releasing my hand and smiling to take the sting out of his words.

With that realization, I set us both free. My mother and me. Free from obligations. Free from expectations. Free to be.

~

*Y*ou know, that *nadi shastra* man had said another thing. He had said that I would lead a tumultuous life, with many twists and turns. The "action" will apparently never stop. He even gave a reason for all this. And the reason was that I had, in my last birth, incurred the wrath of Shiva. I had supposedly been the high-priest of a big Shiva temple in Thanjavur, and a teacher of the Vedas and all. Big time spirituality! But at the height of my power, when people were flocking to me in droves, I had become very arrogant and had intentionally insulted Shiva.

Now, Shiva is the wrong kind of God to choose to insult. One must always try and be in the good books of Shiva. But I, in my last birth, went ahead and insulted him. So he whirled around, did a Cosmic Dance as it were, and cursed me — cursed me for that life and the next. Don't ever fool around with Shiva, I'm warning you. You'll pay the way I'm paying. He'll zap *Shani* down on you and once *Shani* takes up your case — you're finished.

Towards the end of my last life, I had realized the error of my ways and had done various *parihaarams* and *praayschits*. Shiva, being basically benign, softened a bit and added that though I will lead a tumultuous life and will know many disappointments and very little peace of mind, he will always watch over me and bail me out of each crisis. Ever since, I have lived solely on that assurance. *Forward in faith!*

~

I believed in those Matunga prophesies, especially the second one, and still do. No matter how hard I tried to be scientific and logical about this *nadi shastra* business, I was able to brush it aside as jungle-lore only up to a point. Deep down, where logic does not reach, I believed. I know I said somewhere earlier that I have to question everything and cannot accept anything that's been handed down. And I do. But I never said that I was consistent, and that I never contradicted myself. Like everybody else, I too have my Achilles heel — or whatever heel it is — the weak spot. And mine was the Matunga prophesies.

I admit that in the cold light of day, *nadi shastra* is full of holes. It doesn't hold water at all. Are you familiar with this stuff? Apparently, a *rishi* sat down and wrote the life-histories of generations and generations of people, by examining thousands of thumb impressions. He wrote down all these histories on *Olas*, those palm-leaves that look like a folded-up Japanese fan. You have to give the astrologer your date of birth, your name and your thumb impression. If he has your *ola,* he'll read it out to you in high-voltage Tamil. It is possible that your *ola* doesn't exist at all, in which case you're lucky. *I don't know why fortune smiles on some and let's the rest go free-eee….* . There is a song like that!

Before I give you the completely wrong picture, let me assure you that I did not spend all my days brooding over this whole business, like some Edgar Allen Poe character, until I became a shadow of my former self. It's just that I couldn't completely forget about it either. Events kept reminding me of it. I had thought that once I reached Alanghat, things would settle down and I would lead a marvelously boring and uneventful life until I hit ninety-five and am allowed to die. I mean, what can possibly happen in a tiny, single-street village like Kunnathur? For Kunnathur's teenage crowd, going to Cheriathur was a major excitement — Cheriathur with it's bright lights and Typing and Shorthand Institute! And Trichur was considered a bustling metropolis. That's how small Kunnathur was!

~

I was wrong. I had come here to hide but the opposite happened. I actually *emerged*. Within the first few months of my arrival at Kunnathur, I knew I had undergone a transformation. I use the word "transformation" deliberately, knowing that it sounds very dramatic. In my opinion, change in oneself can take place only as a "transformation". It has to be sudden. On the spot. Not planned or phased out. With the desire to change, comes change itself, and in that sense, it *is* a transformation.

Throughout my life, I had felt deeply dissatisfied with myself. I didn't like what I saw in the mirror. It seemed to me as if all the other people in the world were so much more accomplished then I was. I was the failure — the non-starter. Then there were a lot of other niggling little things. My job was not OK. I wasn't being paid enough. I was overweight. India was a useless bloody country. So on and so forth.

I don't know the exact moment when I stopped grappling with all this, but suddenly there were no longer any conflicts. The ones that were there, had became irrelevant. I think what helped to some extent was the fact that I had tipped a lot of the excess baggage overboard. The job and the pay, for example. If I don't have a head, how can I have a headache?! But then again, maybe that wasn't what did the trick. Because as long as I was going round and round in that particular groove, I would always be looking for — and finding — something that would create conflict within me. The right thing to do was to step off. Just step off. That was the answer.

And that is what I did; without ever actually telling myself that that was what I had to do. It happened in the most secret chambers of my being. So deep inside that the stepping-off wasn't even a conscious action. That is why I felt transformed. For the first time ever, I found myself in a limitless silence; at the very core of my being, a wonderful tranquillity. Once I was able to enter that zone of silence, nothing affected me. I wasn't always able to find it though. So I couldn't (and I still can't) enter it at will. But there were times — rare, wonderful times — when I *did* find it. It was like looking down into a vast expanse of clouds.

Those moments gave me a wonderful sense of peace that stayed with me for days together. The memory of those moments was enough to rejuvenate me and so most of the things that happened after moving to Kunnathur, didn't have the power to upset me. At least, not for very long. In that sense, my moving to Kunnathur was a sort of landmark in my life. It was only then that I started seeing a glimmer of light through the thick fog that had surrounded me. I started seeing myself from within, and started accepting what I saw.

~

*B*ut some pretty bizarre things did happen. Of these I shall tell you.

Part Two

Thirteen

Guruvayoor Ekadasi

Kerala has two seasons of rain. The first is in May, when the northwest monsoon winds blow in from the Arabian Sea and the second is in October. The October rains, brought by the northeast winds from the Bay from Bengal, are not as heavy as the ones in June.

The *puzha* had lost its muddy and turbulent look by the time I moved into Alanghat, in late November, after the second monsoon. She was now a greenish blue; calm, benign and sparkling in the sun as if she wore a sequined veil. She was a busy river — at least she always had busy people around her. On her own, perhaps she wasn't all that busy, except for the routine activity of flowing along.

There was a railway bridge running across the *puzha*, out of sight from my back porch. I could hear the trains very clearly though. From any part of the house. The sound of the wheels changed when the train moved onto the bridge — it became hollow and deep — and I could tell the exact moment when, letting out a long whistle, the engine left the bridge on the other side because the sound would change again. The ground seemed to heave beneath my feet whenever a train passed. Back then, one or two goods trains still had steam engines and I would wait for them just to hear the plaintive and lonely sound of the whistle in the quiet peace of the night.

At night the *puzha* looked different — not plump and matronly like she did in the daytime. At night she looked slim and beautiful, as if she had let down her hair for the wind to play with. She was at her best when the moon was full, round and pale yellow in the sky above. On those special nights, she'd dress up in midnight-blue silk and wear her favorite diamonds.

The temple on her other bank, sharply silhouetted in the moonlight, enhanced the air of timelessness that adorned her. Its steps, gleaming white in the moonlight, were a sharp contrast against her own inky depths. Far in the distance, further down the *puzha*, shone a few yellow lights from the houses in the village; the only indication that there were people nearby. Even further down, the chimney of the Standard Brick and Tile Factory towered black against the night sky.

On nights like these, when the moon was full, the trains that passed over the bridge looked mysterious. The glint of metal in the moonlight cast strange reflections in the water below. The change in sound as the wheels rolled onto the bridge, added to the sense of mystery.

One night I saw a passenger train with all its lights on. It appeared suddenly, as if out of nowhere, and thundered across the tracks giving me a fascinating glimpse of its passengers — eating, talking, sleeping, playing cards or just sitting. All in the flash of a second, until the train let out a long whistle and vanished into the night like a phantom.

~

*A*langhat looked resplendent after the face-lift. Her brand-new tiles gleamed in the sun. Her pillars and doors shone richly in the dim, cool interiors and her Magnolia coloured walls were immaculate. All the furniture had been polished and arranged in the rooms on the ground floor. Brass lamps hung in every corner. The lampshades and chandeliers lying in a heap upstairs, had been taken out and fixed. I had re-arranged all the family portraits and had added the four huge Ravi Verma paintings that I had found wrapped up in an old cloth in one of the rooms. They now graced the drawing room, bordered by palms in *varpadam* pot holders. The Alanghat coat-of-arms, now polished and shining, hung at the entrance in its rightful place. Sunshine streamed in through the open windows, merging with the mellow gold of the brass and the cream of the walls, giving the house a warm and friendly look. Yes, she looked beautiful and I could almost see her preening as

THE RIVER HAS NO CAMERA

she admired herself. She didn't look spooky and frightening anymore. In fact, I had slept like a baby on my first night there. All alone.

It was after a very long time that I slept like this — normally, I mean — without any rum or *ganja* or valium. I felt so peaceful and grateful lying there after a good night's sleep, savoring a sense of wellbeing, that I couldn't stop my eyes from filling up. I cried until my nose was blocked and I couldn't breathe. The day was so special for me that I went to the temple and broke a coconut.

I realised how much I had changed, just how far I had come. I started playing my *veena* on the back porch, every morning. I played because I felt like playing. There was nothing forcing me. No compulsion.

The goods train woke me up at 4.30 every morning and so I would sit and play to the *puzha* and to the *devi* across the river, till the skies awakened. They didn't mind - the *puzha* and the *devi* - that I was often off-key and that I sometimes sounded like a Maruti in the reverse gear. I didn't have to apologize. They knew.

My first concert was on *Guruvayoor Ekadasi*. *Ekadasi* is the eleventh day after the *karthavaave*, the dark moon. The third day of the month of *Virchigam* is the *Ekadasi* specific to the Krishna temple at Guruvayoor. It is a day of fasting and prayer — an auspicious day.

That morning the moon was almost full. It hung just above the *peepul* tree near the temple and bathed the entire river in its tranquil, resplendant light. I played the *veena* and sang until the *puzha* changed from silver to molten orange to shimmering blue.

The change was sudden. For a moment the sun was a shy little orange thing peeping out from behind a dark hill and the next minute, it lit up the entire sky — pure, as only the morning sun can be. Suddenly there was colour — the green of the trees, the blue of the water, the flowers, the grass, the stones... each had their own colour, their own shape and their own role to play. Suddenly there was life, in all its triumphant glory. Birds sang, cows lowed and people walked to the river to bathe and offer their thanks for another day, as perfect as the last.

I could see all this from my back porch and it was always cool and beautiful there, no matter what the time. It became my favourite part of the house despite the fact that it was there that Raman Nayar had killed Keshavan Nayar. It was from there that I could see the steps that led to the *puzha*. The steps where Raman Nayar and Keshavan Nayar had fought and where Keshavan Nayar had fallen to his death. I could imagine the scene vividly — Keshavan Nayar falling headlong with a wild cry, his brass *lota* tumbling after him, glistening in the sun and making a loud, raucous noise in a stunning silence, while the whole family stood watching. And now, thirty years later, I sat playing my *veena* in the same porch, in front of the same steps and the same *puzha*.

The same *puzha*? No, I am wrong. She had flowed on and was still flowing. And she will continue to flow long after my time has passed. No, the *puzha* was not the same. The porch was and the steps were.

Whenever I thought about that story, I always ended up thinking about Narayanankutty. What had happened to him? How had he spent all those years in jail? How had he dealt with the horrible truth of having killed a man? Killing a man was bad enough, but added to that was the fact that the man he had killed was his own uncle — the uncle whom he had adored all his life.

Had he repented? Had he sat in his cell and wished he had never picked up that *koduvaal* and followed Raman Nayar? Did his anger vanish the minute the terrible deed was done? Did he miss his uncle and wish he were still alive?

How had my poor, wretched uncle coped all these years? How must he have felt driving a *koduvaal* into a man's stomach, then pulling it out and pushing it in again? Was it easier the third time? Only he would know the answer to that one. And would he ever be able to forget?

What a terrible burden to have to carry. Mine had almost been too much for me. Imagine his! A single act, driven by anger — that's all it took to destroy his entire life. What a frightening thought.

Fourteen

*L*ucky came to live with me about a month after I had moved in. He was a scrawny, black pup with a tail that looked like a dried-up drumstick. I found him near the *Piles and Fistula* signboard. He was sitting and howling in the shade of the *neem* tree. I knew just how he must have felt, having sat and howled (figuratively) exactly as I had, on several occasions. So without giving it a second thought, I picked him up and put him into the back seat of my Trax, feeling a bit like how Shiva must feel each time he looks into my affairs.

I picked up my second waif a month later. Lucky and I were sitting on one of the branches of the mango tree, wondering what to do with ourselves. Getting used to my own company had actually been one of the toughest lessons for me. When I was in Bombay, free time had been anathema. It had to be filled with something —

anything. A movie. A lunch date. Shopping. My mind always shied away from the idea of sitting by myself and enjoying my own company. Enjoying my own company was of course, a distant dream. No, not even a distant dream; it was a dream waiting to be dreamt. Now I had all the free time in the world. And gradually, I had begun to feel comfortable with myself. Sitting alone with myself, was now the same as sitting with someone else.

So, I was sitting in the shade of the mango tree, throwing stones for Lucky, who had blossomed into a furry naughty thing, when Devi entered the courtyard. I watched her walk towards me, idly wondering what she could possibly want. Even before she started to speak, I liked her. Her mouth had a humorous twist to it and her eyes had a perpetually wry expression. She was an agricultural labourer - a field hand — one of the women who had come to clean and weed the grounds when I had first moved in. Although he had never set eyes on her before, Lucky welcomed her as if she were a war hero. He was like that — not much of a watchdog. After he had gone back to his business of fetching stones, she told me her woeful tale and asked me to give her a job.

Her story can be summarized in three words. It was a story that as old as the hills. Pregnant - Unmarried - Destitute.

She moved in that evening and became my housekeeper and cook. I had found my huge kitchen with its ancient stoves completely mystifying and had taken to using my grandmother's makeshift kitchen and a coil stove. With Devi as my instructor, I intended to master the art of cooking on an open fire. That was how we became the three musketeers — rather, the three pariahs. The aristocrat, the pauper and the puppy.

~

*H*er story had, however, given me something to think about. For the first time, I began to see the other side of the peaceful and prosperous town. I began to see the lives of people who lived on the wrong side of the village. The casual labourers, the field hands, the people of low caste – there, I used the terrible 'c' word! Their lives were hell. Especially the lives of the women. They were all unskilled, with large families and no money. Traditionally, these women did all the laborious work like harvesting the paddy, carrying the sheaves, and threshing and separating coconut husk from the fiber. These jobs fetched little in those days — at times, only about fifteen rupees a day.

For several days after Devi had moved in, I kept thinking about these women. I started observing them whenever I passed them on the road — their clothes, their expressions; trying to understand what their lives were all about. But I didn't actually do anything about it until about two months later.

I was returning after a chat with Shailaja and on an impulse, I turned into a road I had never taken before. That was where most of the laborers, casual workers and field hands lived — people like Devi. They all lived in clean houses — very tiny and packed close together. Nearly all of them were thatched shacks. Women

155

sat outside, scrubbing battered aluminum vessels that had turned black with centuries of use. Some of them were cleaning rice while some were just sitting. Snotty-nosed boys were running about, yelling to one another, their shirts held together by a single button and their shorts hanging so low on their hips that they had to keep hitching them up. There were men sitting around too, smoking *beedies*.

~

Kerala's caste structure was no less convoluted than its land system. Not content with merely convoluting it, the *Nambutiris* went a step further by taking the notion of "untouchability" to its logical conclusion. Besides being labeled "untouchables", it was believed that people from low castes could pollute members of high castes, even from a distance. The Brahmins and the high-caste Nayars were the only two "non-polluting" castes. It was the majority of Kunnathur's "polluting" population that lived in these shacks. Most of these people were the *Pulayas* and the *Parayas*, the lowest in the hierarchy, who, during the time Alanghat's flourished, had no choice but to live far away from the village.

The *Nambutiris* had decided that an *Irava* could pollute them from a distance of 24 feet, a *Mukkuvan* from 32 feet, a *Pulaya* from 64 feet and a *Paraya* from 72 feet. When Solomon told me about this the first time, I found it extremely funny — imagine people walking around with measuring tapes! But this was no laughing matter – those who did not keep the appropriate distance could have paid with their lives. At the time Solomon was a child, this incredulous story was actually a cruel reality.

While a low Nayar sub-caste (there are nearly fourteen Nayar sub-castes and a total of about twenty castes in Kerala) was allowed to enter some of the rooms in the house of a high caste, he was forbidden from eating there. Syrian Christians could not go beyond the verandah, an *Irava* could only step into the courtyard surrounding the house and for the *Paraya*, the outer gate was the limit. These three castes were most despised and shabbily treated of all.

At the sight of a high-caste person, the *Paraya* was expected to hide himself in the fields. While addressing a high-caste man, he had to remove his head-cloth and tuck it into his armpit, keep his eyes fixed to the ground, and cover his mouth with his hands (of course, the *Paraya* could not afford to forget to maintain the statutory distance all this while, to spare the poor *Nambutiri* the agony of having to bathe afresh and perform countless ablutions). In speech, he had to be self-deprecatory.

The fallout of not being allowed near the rest of the people was that, in time, the wretched *Parayas* developed a way of talking, which was closer to yelling. In fact, in those days, since nobody could stand very close to anybody, everybody yelled a lot.

Their trials and tribulations of the low-caste people did not end here. They were all bound to specific high-caste households and were always at their beck-and-call. They lived in the perpetual fear of losing their homes as they could be evicted at random. They were not allowed to enter the temple, let alone bathe in the temple tank. Fencing their houses or tiling their roofs was out of question. Neither men nor women could cover their torsos. In fact, nobody from the low caste could cover one's torso while standing before a *Nambutiri* — not even a high-caste Nayar woman.

In 1893, *Ayyankali* - a man from a low caste – decided to protest by not walking, and climbed into a bullock-cart to travel on the public road. But at that time, he was alone in his protest. 1924 saw the beginning of the end of this inhuman social structure. This was also the year of the Vaikom Temple Satyagraha that carried on till late 1925, and in which Gandhi had participated. The outcome was the Travancore Temple Entry Act, which allowed people of all castes to enter the temple. Even though the act was passed much later – in 1936 – the important thing is that it was passed.

This *Satyagraha* was a milestone in the fight for equality and human rights. Even the most rabid and well-entrenched system can be changed once we decide that it has to be done. Today, the old caste system is on the wane. Everybody moves about everywhere and nobody yells. However, if you scratch the surface you can still see traces of it. A *Paraya* labourer will today, lean against the gate of the landlord's house, cross his legs, look somewhere else and talk. The landlord might even invite him in but will expect the invitation to be politely turned down.

Ordinary people have, by and large, dismantled a centuries-old social structure that had once paralysed their psyche. This makes Kerala unique in comparison it with other caste-ridden states like Bihar. While the caste structure is on its way out, poverty continues to plague the state and is there for all to see. And all this happened within a space of thirty years — the same thirty years that brought down the curtains on Alanghat.

~

I drove the Trax down the road where people had slowly begun to line up. Men, women and children. I felt like a minister; only these people were not shouting slogans and waving banners. They just stood staring at me curiously. Boldly, I drove out of the area, following a bumpy track and finally got on to the main road. All the thoughts I'd had during the last two months finally crystallized into an idea.

The idea was simple enough. I planned to start a support centre in Alanghat for women labourers, along the lines of a co-operative society; a place where they could leave their toddlers and pre-schoolers while they were out at work; a place that would provide them a good meal after a hard day's work; a place that would organise health education for their children; a centre that could inform them of their rights; a place where the women could meet regularly to discuss their problems and find collective solutions; and a forum that would help them manage their finances and save their earnings. Eventually, I wanted it to be run by them. In short,

I envisaged a sort of movement that would not just help them but would empower them and make them independent, aware and articulate — a force to be reckoned with, not a mere bunch of pushovers.

When I first arrived in Kerala, women's paid labour accounted for 44% of the agricultural labour in the state. Also, women had fewer average days of employment in the agricultural sector than men did. It was during the sowing and harvesting season that most women found work, and even then they were paid the lowest wages and given the most unhealthy of jobs, which often entailed long hours of stooping, bending and standing ankle-deep in dirty water — barefoot.

A lot of land-owners in those days used to grumble about the non-availability of labour during the sowing season. This was the major topic of discussion when I first arrived and it still is. That and the rains. It was around this time that a lot of labourers left their villages in search of greener pastures and sought work in towns. Many of them made a beeline for the Gulf, but these were mostly the men. The women stayed behind and their lot didn't change much – the Gulf boom did not change their lives. Despite their meagre education, most of them could read and write; and in spite of the welfare schemes floated by successive governments, these women remained wretchedly poor without a support group of their own.

Sometimes I wonder why I started *Sakhi*, which is what the centre came to be known as. I was bored. Having come out of that withdrawn, morose state I was in when I first came to Kunnathur, I was feeling active and needed something to do. Watering my coconut trees was no longer enough. That could have been one reason, the second reason being that my own experience had taught me something. I had learnt to be self-reliant, bold and fearless, and I could not identify with the way in which these women had painted themselves into a corner. I wanted them to be much more than economic problems or statistics. I wanted them to be human beings, with as great a need to laugh and sing as the rest of us. They no longer needed to accept their lot meekly. They needed to fight, take a stand.

~

I started going to their houses more often — just to talk to them, to make friends with them, to see things from their point of view. They were not "simple", rustic people, with hearts of gold. They were as shrewd as the rest of us, if not more. It took me a long time to explain to them that I was not going to gift them money every month. I was going to help them look after whatever they earned so that they earned more and could then look after themselves. To begin with, I didn't make much headway because the concept was difficult to explain, but I kept at it anyway, sometimes half-heartedly and sometimes with renewed vigor. I was playing it by the ear, waiting for a sign — an indication. I didn't know what the indication would actually be but I knew that I would recognise it when it was time.

As it turned out, the indication was loud and clear, and it carried a placard around its neck. It came in the form of a visitor. Her name was Parameshwari and she came to Alanghat to see me, by herself. She had understood something of what I was trying to tell them. After spending two evenings explaining the whole scheme to her, I asked her to speak to the other women and ask them if they would like to start a group. It was a slow, uphill task, with me having to repeat myself over and over again, as different women came with the same doubts. Once they came to know that Parameshwari had actually come to Alanghat to see me, they all came. Sometimes alone and sometimes in droves.

~

*I*n the month of February, *Kumbham maasam*, soon after the harvest of the *Kanni* crop, we had our first meeting under the mango tree. I don't remember much about what actually happened at that meeting. What I remember most clearly is that Lucky barked at a bald woman throughout the session. He went berserk barking his head off if she so much as shifted in her place.

About thirty women attended the meeting. Parameshwari was of course there, wearing a *muttai* pink blouse, or *bodeece* as they call it. She, for a reason that confused and eluded me completely, kept repeating everything I said in a louder voice. I was relieved when one of the older women told her to shut up, saying that none of them were deaf and were quite capable of hearing and understanding what the *tamburatti* was saying.

This older lady, Narayani, together with Parameshwari and Devi formed a core-group that helped me get the other women together and organize them. In fact, after a while Narayani became the master of ceremonies at those weekly meetings, for which I was extremely thankful.

After four meetings, which left me physically exhausted and completely bewildered, we finally drew up a chart which outlined the more comfortable months, the lean months and the famine-ridden months. Also, after going round and round for a long time — a thing I am used to now but which used to make me want to scream back then — we also decided to start a crèche for the infants and pre-schoolers and a dinner mess for the women. We also decided to start a chit fund, with me as the manager. The main purpose of this fund was that loans up to thousand rupees could be given to any woman in the group, provided her credit rating was high and provided some other woman in the group was willing to nominate her. The other woman wasn't eligible for a loan until this money had been returned — free of interest, of course.

I had planned initially to start this centre with a seed grant from my father and then make it financially self-sufficient over the years, by introducing income-generating schemes through which the women could earn additional money and the centre could get funds to continue its work. And so, *Sakhi* started work, thirteen years

ago. It became a Trust a year later and five years later, its appeal
for financial support was accepted by a British donor agency.

~

*I*f you were to visit Alanghat today, you would see an immense
hustle and bustle. One side of the compound wall has a garage
capable of housing the five jeeps, four scooters and the mini bus
that *Sakhi* owns. My old Trax is gone.

The dining hall has been extended. It now has a Training Centre,
an auditorium, three dormitories, the mess, the kitchen and a reading
room. The crèche has its own building with a playground. All the
buildings have been constructed with bricks and tiles in the Laurie
Baker style that blends with the old house and the surrounding
landscape. An architect in Trichur offered to design them for us.

The first and second floor of Alanghat houses our offices. *Sakhi*
now employs twenty-five full-time people. It has a computer centre,
two telephones and a conference room. I am now the Executive
Director and I have my own separate office in a corner. I attend
only to our most important visitors. For all other visitors, there
are the respective department heads. Sometimes, when I have the
time, I find myself looking out of the window and wondering how
this happened. How did I become so important? How is it that I
now have to wait for monthly reports to find out what's happening
in *Sakhi*? Had it *really* grown so big? I hardly ever meet the women
anymore. I stopped the moment I suspected the program support

staff resented it. These days I meet them only on festivals or celebrations.

Today, I spend most of my time corresponding with the funding agency, the Government and the Press — that is when I am in Alanghat. Otherwise, I am out attending workshops and speaking at seminars; or doing the job I dread the most — signing cheques and authorizing vouchers. They are already discussing the question of leadership. *After me, who?*

~

*Y*es, *Sakhi* has grown now. It's not my little baby anymore. It works in twenty villages, runs a crèche and a dinner mess for groups of three villages, nutrition courses, primary health awareness camps, community credit programs, silk-farming units, and a dairy. It also has a scholarship for girls to get a college education or training in some vocation. It runs a pickle, ready-made *masala* and a hair-oil manufacturing unit which employs two hundred and seventy five people all round the year, except during the harvest and the sowing season when all our members are busy in the rice fields.

Sakhi now has a membership of twenty thousand, of which four hundred and fifty full-time members are men! Apart from British funding, *Sakhi* receives donations from five thousand individuals on a regular basis, which forms the fund that runs the scholarship program. My first donor was Karunakaran, the station master at Cheriathur. Binkity. The Trust also owns 60 acres of land outside Kunnathur where we plan to move our entire operations. But that will take time. Perhaps another ten years.

~

*B*ut all this is *now*, thirteen years later. Back then, in *Kumbham maasam*, on that warm night beneath the mango tree in full bloom, filling the air with its tangy fragrance, all I had was a gaggle of women sitting in my courtyard and shouting at each other in Malayalam.

Fifteen

About two weeks after that first meeting under the mango tree, the memory of which will forever be fragrant with the scent of the mango flowers, the dinner mess got off to a shaky start in Alanghat's dining hall. After three weeks of backbreaking labour, during which time I had yelled myself hoarse and developed a perpetually harassed expression, I decided that I needed help.

To rope in Shailaja was easy. It was Solomon that I was worried about. He was a bit of an enigma, that man. I could never predict his reactions. Look at the time he sent me off, refusing to tell me Alanghat's story and refusing to tell me why he was refusing, only to bring himself all the way to Kunnathur, eight days later at five in the morning, to tell me the same story, which for equally mystifying reasons he now felt I must know. I am not saying there was no method in the man's madness. I'm merely saying that I couldn't readily spot it at that time.

I drove to Manuthy early one morning, canceling the day's performance for the *puzha* and the *devi*. Solomon was sitting on the porch and reading the *Mathrubhumi*. He was the sort, the same sort as my father, who reads the newspaper from the beginning to the end — even the bit about the fall in the price of *jeera*. Not only did he sit and read all that, he also sat and mulled over it. I have seen him do that.

He watched me jump out of the Trax and walk up to him. His eyes lit up as I drew near, and a faint smile crept upon his face. He took his time folding the paper carefully and deliberately, put it aside and turned in his chair so that he was facing me. I had his complete attention. That is another thing I liked about him — his way of making me feel that everything I had to say was important, more important than anything he might be doing at that time.

I told him of my activities of the last month. He listened with a look of pride in his eyes, a look I was not accustomed to. Nobody had ever been proud of me before — but then I don't suppose I had ever done anything to make people proud of me. It made me feel shy and self-conscious. I ended my tirade by asking him if he would come and help.

A slight change came over him when I suggested that. A marked change actually. I could sense it immediately, and my heart sank. Why didn't he want to help? I sat looking at him anxiously, waiting for him to say something. He withdrew deep into himself and his eyes moved away from me. He seemed to gaze at a place only he could see. Then he turned to me and said a very funny thing. 'I'll have to help.' After a long pause, he added in a whisper, '*Vidhi*'. What did he mean by that? He didn't *have* to help. Nobody *had* to do anything! There were times when I found Solomon very exasperating.

~

*A*ll the way down to Alanghat he sat half turned in his seat, watching me drive. I showed off my driving skills, making it all look very difficult and complicated; and that brought the slight smile on again. He knew I was showing off and I got the impression that that was what he wanted me to do. He wanted to see how well I could drive.

I showed him around Alanghat, resplendent after the renovation. I told him about how wonderful things used to be long ago, and how rich we were. He followed me around the place, looking dutifully at whatever I pointed, his hand reaching out to touch - almost caress - a pillar here and a banister there. The woodwork looked beautiful after its fresh coat of varnish, and the slight smile never left his face as he listened to my endless chatter. I was getting quite carried away with my stories and I even made up a few of my own about my mother and Narayanankutty (now that I knew he existed!). He listened to all that too, his smile just a little bit wider.

Finally, we stopped in front of the picture gallery. It was here that I really let my imagination soar. I hadn't the faintest idea who all those people in the photographs and paintings were, but that didn't stop me from shooting off. By the time I finished, his shoulders were shaking with laughter. How well he understood me!

~

*T*hat night I wrote a long letter to my father, telling him that I was not returning to Bombay and that I was very happy in Kunnathur. I told him about the centre and my plans for it. In the end, I asked him for twenty thousand rupees. There's no harm in *asking*, is there?

I didn't know what sort of a response my letter would get — and I prepared myself for a nasty one. When it came, there was a draft for twenty five thousand enclosed. Also attached was a detailed description of the books of accounts I would have to maintain and suggestions about how I could make the project financially self-sufficient in the near future. My mother had also written — a hesitant letter asking me why I had been so silent for so long and when I would get my phone connection. There was also a cryptic warning about the dangers of washing my hair very late at night. I read her letter over and over again, missing her and wanting to see her again. Even if it were only to have yet another fight.

I gave my father's letter to Solomon to read. He took two hours to read a letter I had taken five minutes to read! He sat out, under the mango tree, and read it there all by himself. He returned it to me and asked me, sort of hesitantly, what my mother had written. I handed the other letter too. He stood holding the folded letter, rubbing it between his thumb and fingers for a minute before opening and reading it. Then he went into the room I had converted into an office and followed my father's instructions right down to the last detail. That's how we got our first entry for 25,000 in our books. And our first Treasurer.

~

*T*here were now seven of us to do all the work. Solomon's wife, Saramma, Shailaja, Devi, me and the four other women I had employed for the job. It was a happy time for all of us, especially for Shailaja and me. We were the ones who went on a shopping spree armed with a long list, giggling helplessly over everything.

We didn't limit ourselves to the list. Solomon was most surprised to see us return with two calves — a fawn coloured one and a glistening black one. We couldn't resist their eyes, you see. Soft and shy. We weren't able to explain very clearly to Solomon why we had decided to buy them. We could hardly tell him about the eyes. He was such a stingy old man — so fussy about money that he just refused to sanction a payment. If we had told him that we couldn't walk away from those eyes, back they would have gone that very day. Shailaja was worse than I was. She said it was their eyes, their ears, their noses and the nape of their necks.

But those two calves proved very useful later on as they were the beginning of the fairly big dairy we run today. We named them Nidhi and Amba and spent the next morning bathing them and tying coloured threads between their horns and bells around their necks. And kissing them on their noses, which exasperated Solomon like anything. Shailaja went a little mad and insisted that we do an *aarti* for them, which made Solomon turn and walk away, to show his disapproval. Nidhi and Amba spent four days under the mango tree, while a shed was constructed for them in the backyard. And that was when Pudukolen joined us to look after Nidhi and Amba. I think he is the only one who is still with us from the old lot. Even Devi has left. She got married last year, to a cobbler in Cheriathur.

~

*T*here was a lot of work for all of us. Solomon's wife and Devi looked after the crèche we had started on the first floor and that kept them busy all day, leaving the five of us to manage the dinner mess. Solomon helped but he was very slow, and he had to keep adjusting his glasses so that he could see properly, taking nearly twenty minutes to peel one potato. However, before the work became too much for us to handle, more women came forward to help us. Gradually, they shed their inhibitions and began to treat the centre as their own. They cleaned the dining hall, washed the vessels, helped cut vegetables or clean rice. They planned a roster for themselves, allotting each person a specific day in the week to work as volunteer. They started spending all their free time there, with their children. That was when I started the journal club — that's what I called it; the women didn't call it anything. We started with reading the daily newspaper and commenting on the news. The women would take turns to read, sitting in a circle in the dining hall. Lucky would attend too. He was practically a founder member. He'd stretch out in the centre of the circle, and by the time the reader of the day had spelled her way through the first line, he'd be twitching and fast asleep. I wonder what dogs dream of when they sleep — they seem to have such a good time! I think I'd like to be a dog in my next birth.

From there we progressed to reading magazines. After many months, the group evolved into a sort of study circle where, after Janaki joined us — she was a retired school- teacher— we read books like *Indulekha. Indulekha* is a classic, the first Malayalam novel written by O. Chandu Menon, in 1899.

The meetings under the mango tree also began to assume a sort of pattern. First we clapped hands and sang songs, then the arguments began, and finally, when all of us had yelled ourselves hoarse, we'd get down to business.

One of the first things we did was to open a savings bank account for each of the members at the Nedungadi Bank. Mr. Baby, the manager, would attend the meetings in the first week of every month and collect their money. Nearly all the women put something aside. It was forced saving — they didn't really have anything to put aside. These savings were to build up the community credit fund.

~

*S*olomon had been giving my father's suggestion that we raise our own funds in order to make the place self-sufficient, a great deal of thought. Finally he came up with the idea of making hair oil and selling it in Trichur. I used to make oil for the hair, with leaves and flowers — a recipe that had been handed down from generation to generation in my family. It even figured in Rugmani Devi Amma's cookbook. Solomon felt there would be a big market for it. So Shailaja and I pulled out of the kitchen and with Solomon's help we started on the hair oil while Pudukolen was put in charge of our nursery. We started with fifty bottles.

On Nandu's advice, we decided to sell the hair oil in Trichur rather than Palghat. He said that Trichur had bigger shops, richer people, and a large Christian population. He said that Christians were the ones with style, not Nayars — *Christianmaar de adayil ullu stylum karyangalam okhe* — and that they had a greater understanding of charity. We took Nandu's word for it because he owned a grocery store and we felt he would know best. You may well ask how a man who owned a *kirana* store in a remote town like Kunnathur would know anything about a launching a hair oil (I believe management schools devote an entire course to the subject of product launches), but he was all we had and we were grateful for him.

So, early one morning, I drove to Trichur with my fifty bottles rattling in the back seat, proceeding on the dim theory that if I could get ten stores to keep the oil on a consignment basis, things would work out. They did!

Our herbal hair oil became quite popular; but our nursery could not give us the amount of leaves and flowers we needed to increase production. In a sense, it was good because the demand was always more than the supply and we had a long waiting list. That in turn ensured that most of our customers were regular buyers. Most of them were affluent women, and so we were able to price it quite high. One of these women was married to Trichur's leading architect and he came forward to help us design the campus, many years later, when we were expanding the centre.

However, at that time, the money coming in from the sale of hair oil was not enough. What we needed was a constant flow of revenue, and so we expanded our "product line" to include pickles, meat *masala*, *sambhar masala* and a face scrub — a hotchpotch of products, but who cared! Even then, we barely broke even. It was to take us four years to make the production unit profitable. Only after that did it start generating some revenue for the centre.

By then, the State Government was funding the dinner mess under one of its welfare schemes. A year later, we were being funded by a British donor agency. Although we didn't really need to run the production unit once foreign funds started coming in, we didn't shut it down. And I don't mind telling you that the only reason I kept at it, despite the losses it incurred during the first four years, was because it had been Solomon's idea. And that really was the only reason. There were times when everything and everybody was screaming at me, telling me that it was not worth the heartache, but I just couldn't do it.

~

*W*ithin a year of starting the centre, we were all working twelve hours a day and a number of women from the group were volunteering to help us. I was averaging four trips a week to Trichur, and beginning to feel like a truck driver. We worked in a perpetual state of confusion, where nobody had a clear idea as to what was actually going on. And we sometimes lost sight of the overall picture, which was good in a way because the overall picture was initially quite dismal — with the number of women joining the centre growing at an alarming rate, a pittance for an income, and the monsoon - the starving months - looming ahead.

It was around this time, about a year after we had started the centre, that Muthote Shankaran Nayar came to Alanghat to visit me.

Sixteen

Shivarathri

I had never stopped to consider the reaction of the Kunnathur elite to my scheme. I knew that Nandu approved because his wife was right there beside me the whole day, along with her children. Nandu would himself bear the expenses of the special monthly treat of *pereppu payasam* and steamed bananas. I knew Binkity approved because he would donate a hundred rupees every month. I knew that Doctor Krishnankutty approved because he had held two camps at Alanghat and had studied in detail the causes of skin infections and worms. He also taught us the basics of hygiene and dental care. All the women and children were checked for worms, skin infections, lice, eye diseases and dental problems. We didn't have to worry about immunisation because the women were quite aware of that and in any case, Kunnathur had a Primary Health Care centre. It was routine health care, sanitation and hygiene that had to be tackled.

I had the support of these three people but I had no clue as to what the rest of the village was saying. I would have gone on, supremely unconcerned, had Muthote Shankaran Nayar not visited me.

~

*I*t was on a Sunday that he visited me. I was sitting in the front porch with my *veena*. My playing had certainly improved — all that remained were a few jagged edges. I had come a long way but I hadn't quite reached *there* yet. I can't explain what I mean by *there*. Perhaps a state of mind would explain it best. Sometimes — maybe twice — I came somewhere close to close (*somewhere close to close* but not close) when I sensed faintly what it could be like over *there* … across. And even that lasted only for a second — the briefest instant. But that didn't disappoint me. Look how far I had come!

I looked up and saw Shankaran Nayar as he entered the *padipera*, the gatehouse. He was a stocky man with a lot of hair on his face. His eyebrows were hairy, his ears were hairy, even his nostrils were hairy. The hair on his head was dyed black and it stood in ridges, not moving at all. I think it would have remained like that — set in concrete — even if he was caught in a blizzard, a sandstorm and a typhoon all rolled into one. He had a perpetually sarcastic expression and a way of drawing back his lips when he spoke that was very irritating.

He was the *Panchaayat* President and lived in a purple-coloured house in Cheriathur. He had another year as President, before the next election was due. That was all I knew about him. He had come to see me along with another man called V.K. Menon when I was staying with Shailaja. Throughout the visit he sat silently, smoothing the hair on the back of his head, and the only time he opened his mouth was to say something to V.K. Menon, which I did not understand. There were no words in what he said. It sounded like '*Aaaaiye*'. Does that make sense to you? He said that when I was briefly describing my plans for Alanghat to them.

I watched him walk up to the house, wondering why he had come to see me. I invited him in and went into the kitchen to ask Lakshmi, Devi's mother, to make some coffee. Devi had delivered a baby boy four months ago. When she had been about seven months pregnant, Lakshmi had come to see her and had attempted to patch things up with her daughter. I had employed her too. She was in the kitchen now, cutting vegetables.

~

I went back into the porch, feeling vaguely apprehensive. We talked about the rains and the government. Polite, banal conversation. Devi came in with the coffee. He watched her as she kept the tray down on the table, a sneer widening his nostrils and making the hair inside stick straight out. Then he watched her leave the porch and go back inside. I gestured to the cup placed in front of him, inviting him to drink but he didn't touch it. I picked mine up, sensing that things were about to go wrong and reminded myself to stay calm. I turned away from him slightly, to face the breeze that was blowing in from the courtyard. Seeing me sit there, drinking my coffee and apparently enjoying the breeze, he widened his nostrils even further and drew back his lips and rolled his head, as if to tell me, 'Can't you see that I'm sneering at you.' I continued to sip my coffee.

He leaned back in chair and asked me in a supercilious, amused sort of way why I had kept 'that slut and her bastard' in my house. But I knew that he wasn't amused at all. He was mad as hell. 'This isn't Bombay,' he said. 'This is Kunnathur and respectable people live here.' What did I mean by allowing all these amoral *Pulayas* into my house? Didn't I understand the disgrace I was bringing upon respectable people? 'These low-castes don't know the meaning of the word gratitude', he said. 'They' would become insufferable and all Kunnathur would be ruined forever because of me.

He didn't stop there. Devi, he said, had slept with every man there was in Kunnathur. Did I know that? I stared at him while he spoke, forcing myself to slowly sip my coffee. I knew that unnerved him. Unwittingly, I had found my weapon. I didn't have very much coffee left in my cup but I sipped along, with a knot in my throat and my shoulders stiff. I put down the cup when he had finished, then stood up and asked him if he would like to see the child.

Perhaps he would be able to tell if it was his and that way we would be able to rule out at least one man in Kunnathur.

He sprang up, pushing his chair back with such force that it slid all the way to the end of the porch and fell, and started shouting. The veins in his forehead looked swollen and his face looked purple and mottled, against his dyed hair.

'I came here to try and make you understand things because you are young — not to be insulted.' He took a deep breath, then resumed waving his hands about and shouting. 'And if you think that by living with all these low-caste people and getting their support, you'll become the next President, you're wrong. You Alanghat people are all *kacheras. Varam Kacheras.*' He used *Kacheras*, the Hindi word for rubbish. 'Don't we know what you are? The whole *panchaayat* knows. Murderers and drunks! *Praandermaar*!' Mad people.

He barged out, kicking Lucky out of his way, baring his thick hairy legs, his *mundu* flying in the wind.

~

*W*hen I sat down in front of the *veena* again, my mind was a complete blank. I felt all knotted up inside and too agitated to sit still. I got into the Trax and drove off, with Lucky sitting next to me looking very sorry for himself. Without making a conscious decision, I drove to the *Shiva Kshetram* in Thripallur. The temple grounds were deserted except for a white ambassador parked in the shade of a *bilva* tree. I got out leaving Lucky in the Trax, but he began howling when he realised that I was planning to leave him alone. So we sat together in the shade of the big *peepul* tree, enjoying the breeze and listening to the soothing sound of *peepul* leaves rustling in the wind. We were sitting there, Lucky wondering why he was kicked and me watching the way his eyebrows twitched in the breeze, when we saw Aaftab.

He was walking out of the temple, and even from that distance, I could sense a radiance about him. He bent down to pick up a small bag he had left at the entrance, along with his footwear — but he picked it up upside down, and as he walked towards his car, its contents kept falling out one by one. He kept saying 'Oops!' each time something fell. Eventually, he did finally manage to straighten his bag and that's when he saw Lucky and me gawking at him. Changing direction, he walked towards us as if it was the most natural thing to do, while I sat watching him overcome by a strange feeling of *déjà vu.*

He wasn't tall but there was something magical in his short frame — all the way from his toes upwards. He smiled as he reached us — a very sinful smile. I looked up and found myself looking into the eyes of a four-year-old. Big and dark, and gleaming — like *jamuns* on a white plate.

I smiled back. But it felt like a foolish smile. The breeze ruffled his glistening, unruly hair. He pushed it back and asked me, 'Would you by any chance know the way to Kunnathur.' I said hoarsely that I was from there and that he could follow my Trax while I drove back. He laughed and I heard church bells. 'That's wonderful! Maybe you could show me where Alanghat is. There is someone I would like to meet there.' Suddenly the church bells were interrupted by kettledrums. He was here to meet me. He had come all the way from heaven only to meet me! He stretched his hand to scratch Lucky, who melted that very instant. He lay down and surrendered, his ears plastered down and his tail tapping the ground.

'A man named Mr. Solomon. Do you know him?'

The bells and drums stopped abruptly. Back to the good old *peepul* leaves. He wanted to see Solomon. *Solomon!* I told him that Solomon lived in Manuthy and not in Kunnathur.

'Then maybe I can meet the lady who lives there. Do you — ' He broke off and looked intently at me for a second. 'You are her, aren't you?'

~

I floated back to Kunnathur, Muthote Shankaran Nayar completely forgotten. And two hours after my first visitor had stalked out, flashing his ugly legs at me, I was once again sitting in my porch, offering another cup of coffee to my second visitor of the day.

And how different the second visitor was! Suddenly I was aware of the peace of that February afternoon and the isolation of my house on the hill. I was at ease and happy, as if I was meeting an old friend after a long time, and there was so much I wanted to ask and so much I wanted to say. I remember we laughed a lot that day, and talked endlessly. I did something I had never done before. I brought out my *veena* and played a *kirtana* in *Raaga Saaveri* for him, without him asking me to do so. Not a very difficult thing to do but I *did* it, and that's the important thing.

But that was not all I did. That night, before going to bed, I pruned my eyebrows a bit and did something about the hair on my arms, which had grown unhindered for two years. So now you know just how impressed I was!

~

*A*aftab was a photojournalist based in Bombay and he was working on a series of articles on *Shaivism,* Shiva worship, in South India. He had come to Trichur to visit the Mammiyur *Shiva Kshetram*, an ancient temple very close to Guruvayur. The story goes that long ago, when the temple was thriving, a priest at the Mammiyur *Kshetram* was very rude to an old man who had come there asking food, whereupon the old man told the priest that he would go to the nearby Guruvayur. At the time, Guruvayur was a small temple where no one ever bothered to go. But soon after the incident between the priest and the old man, Mammiyur's fortunes fell while Guruvayur became popular. The old man was 'none other than Krishna', Aaftab declared dramatically, wide-eyed and waving his hands about. Though the temple is no longer what it used to be, it was still very beautiful and had made a significant contribution to the rise of *Shaivism* in Kerala. It also had a stock of interesting stories, like the one Aaftab had told me, and that is why he had included it in his research.

~

*W*hile in Trichur, he had stayed with a family known to some friends of his in Bombay. They had told him about the work we were doing at Alanghat. Since he had a couple of days before moving on, he had borrowed a car and driven over with the intention of meeting us, making a brief halt at Thripallur, where there was another ancient Shiva temple.

He didn't tell me all this in at once. I pieced his story together as we walked the grounds and talked. The other things I found out were that he and I were had gone to the same school, that he had lived a ten-minutes drive away from my Worli flat, that we were partial to onion *sambhar* and that we had lived in the US for seven years. And, like me, he too wasn't married.

We had onion *sambhar* for lunch that afternoon, and since we did not have much to do, we drove down to Nandu's house and from there to Solomon's house. After tea, Aaftab got into his Ambassador and drove back to Trichur. I wondered if I would ever see him again. I thought of him all evening, until I fell asleep that night, happy to have met him. While talking to him, I realized that my disjunct memory of Bombay had revived once again. Meeting him had made me nostalgic and I almost felt like visiting Bombay again.

The next day was *Shivarathri*. Early that morning I drove back to the Shiva *Kshetram* in Thripallur. I stood in front of the idol for a long time but I had no prayer to say. What had I come here for? What did I want? I stood there with my hands folded, oblivious of the priest walking in and out of the inner sanctum, wearing only a wet piece of cloth, and tried to make sense of how I was actually feeling. I tried to articulate the reason for my being there.

A woman brushed past, wearing a brown nylon sari and smelling vaguely of Chandrika soap and turmeric. She was carrying a black handbag that had the white plastic handle of a folding umbrella sticking out. She also carried her lunch in a round steel tiffin-box and a notebook and in her other hand. *Thayar saadam* — curd rice and lime pickle, I decided. Her hair was wet and untied but the ends were gathered together in a knot. Two machine-cut gold bangles clinked as she raised a hand to ring the bell. She was muttering something — her prayers, I suppose — under her breath. There were two men standing there as well; their hands clasped under their noses as they stared devotedly into the dark sanctum, lit only by lamps. Unlike me, all these people seemed to know why they were there and what they had to say. Their lips continued to move while their eyes were half shut.

Once again, I went over all the possible reasons for being there. I was happy to have met Aaftab and I knew that Shiva had something to do with it. But that couldn't be the reason I was there. As I've told you earlier, I had a strong belief that Shiva had a lot to do with everything that has ever happened to me — there was a constant interaction and dialogue between us. No, I had not gone there to pray that things should work out between Aaftab and me. I would have been happy if they did but if they did not, I was quite willing to accept that too. It was not something I wanted to pray for. That couldn't be it. Suddenly I felt foolish standing there in front of a dark, cavernous room, with my hands folded. There was no Shiva here, in this heap of stones.

If only someone could tell me why I had come! Something had compelled me to drive all the way to this temple. What? Was it the temple — was it Shiva, who is supposed to inhabit this temple? Had Shiva called me? Or did I want to call on Shiva? *Did I?*

Perhaps I did. My scattered mind became more focussed. I had come here to make an important call. Thripallur was like a pay phone from where I could make a long-distance call. I reassured myself that my words were irrelevant. It did not have to be a proper prayer in Sanskrit. *Omkaaram bindu sanyuktam* — what's the next line? I could say *Nani teri morni ko more lay gayee*, if that was all I could think of. I didn't think Shiva would mind.

My eyes closed and when the prayer came, it came from deep within my soul. And it wasn't *Nani teri morni* ... . It was a *sthuti* that my *bhagvathar* had taught me. See, I do know proper Sanskrit prayers after all! I don't know where that *sthuti* came from and why it was hiding there for so long. But it came and my voice sounded deep and resonant.

Prabhum praan natham
Vibhum vishwanatham
Jagannath natham
Sadaanandbhaajam
Bhavathbhavya bhuteshwaram bhutnatham
Shivam Shankaram
Shambhum ishaanmidhe… .

I opened my eyes slowly. I didn't know when, if ever, I would pray again but for the time being that was enough. I had reached out. I turned to leave and noticed in passing that everybody else in the temple, including the priest were standing frozen — surprised . A small boy had his mouth open. I smiled at them and walked out with a skip in my step.

~

*T*hat day was a Monday, the day I usually went to the bank. As I drove there, I passed V.K. Menon on the way. Monday was his post-office day. I waved to him as I drove by and waited for him to return the wave, as was the routine. But that day he did not wave. He just looked down and quickened his pace. It made me frown. V.K. Menon was a good friend of Muthote Shankaran Nayar. Perhaps Muthote Shankaran Nayar had told him about his visit to Alanghat.

I swung the Trax off the road and parked at my usual spot some distance from the bank. There was no change in Mr. Baby's manner towards me but then I had a big account with him. I sat with him for some time, withdrew some money and left. The stairs leading to the bank were narrow and built against the outer wall of the building. The wall was painted bright yellow and it had a broad red arrow pointing the way up the stairs. The other side of the staircase was unprotected. I walked down carefully using the wall as a support.

When I reached the Trax I got the shock of my life. Pieces of glass lay all over the place, reflecting the bright sunlight like bits of mica. The windshield, the windows, the rear view mirrors – everything had been smashed. I looked at the small teashop nearby. A couple of men stood around, their oily heads glistening in the sunshine, but the idiots looked studiously away. And though they didn't have to say, I knew this was the work of *Muthote* Shankaran Nayar.

~

*T*his was the first time I had experienced such violence — such hatred — directed straight at me and I stood there trembling like a leaf. I found a cloth under the seat and tried to wipe the seat and the hood of the Trax but my hands were shaking badly. I knew those men in the shop were watching and it made me self-conscious. After some time, I gave up. I climbed in and sat down, not caring if I were sitting on broken glass. I took a deep breath, started the Trax and drove away, thankful that the Trax had behaved well and not let me down in front of those men.

By the time I reached Alanghat the fear had gone. I swerved into the big gates and screeched to a halt, an inch from Solomon who was standing under the mango tree. He didn't jump out of the way, I noticed. Just continued to stand there. Behind him — praise the Lord — was Aaftab!

I climbed out of the Trax and walked towards them. Seeing the state of the Trax, Solomon's first thought was that I had been in an accident. When I told him what had happened the day before and this morning, he looked worried. The lines on his face suddenly deepened. He sighed and walked slowly back to the house.

Aaftab had been standing silently to one side all this while. I turned towards him and smiled. He smiled back, as openly and sinfully as he had done the day before.

Seventeen

*A*aftab stayed for a little more than a month. After a couple of days of driving back and forth between Trichur and Kunnathur, he gratefully accepted Nandu's invitation to stay at his place. Nobody had asked him to stay on in Kunnathur and nobody asked him when he was going to leave. We accepted him unconditionally — no questions asked, and soon he became part of the 'gang', as it were.

When the *chekken* - fellow - who attended at Nandu's store ran away with the tailor's daughter, Aaftab sat at the shop for a whole week. He dutifully measured out *kappala malagu, tore pereppu* - red chillies - and *tur dal* in Nandu's ancient balance — the quarter kilo weight being a stone — wrapping them up into conical bundles in old newspaper and tying them up with brown thread. Once, as I drove past on my way to Trichur, I saw him standing on top of the counter, engrossed in rearranging the buckets and brooms that hung from hooks in the front of the store.

All the same, notwithstanding the sport he'd been, he looked very relieved when the *chekken* came back, with his lawfully wedded wife in tow and asked to have his job back.

~

*A*lthough the centre had been running for a year now, it had not taken on a definite shape. Most of the time we were fighting and everything was very makeshift. I mean, how do I explain the fact that my women's support group now had ten full-time male members? I didn't even know how many people were employed on a full-time basis at the centre and how many were volunteers.

When the number of members started growing at an alarming rate and we began to feel that the women should have a sense of responsibility about the centre, we introduced a monthly fee of twenty rupees. It was supposed to be a deterrent to those who wanted a free ride. That fee was beginning to give me nightmares. None of them paid regularly and on time. In fact, some of them even stopped paying because I hadn't made it compulsory. We now had active accounts for each woman because nearly all of them had unpaid dues. Also, at meal times I sometimes saw women who were not part of the group. They had never registered and nor did they attend the meetings. They would just turn up with their children for a 'free' meal, when they pleased. It was not a free meal – nothing in the centre was supposed to be free. Yes, things were definitely getting out of hand.

Having attended so many meetings and after having lived among the women for more than a year now, I was beginning to realise that there had to be more to the work we were doing than running a dinner mess and fighting under the mango tree. I had to understand the 'economics' of poverty and explain it to them if I had to be of any support to them, if I had to empower them, if I had to make them able to change the quality of their own lives.

No longer could I just stand and stir a big pot of bubbling *sambhar*, muttering incantations (whenever I made *sambhar*, I would always imagine I was a witch. I would hold the ladle with both hands, stir the thick gravy as it bubbled and mutter under my breath.). I needed a plan of action. Ideas were sprouting like beans in my head. I was beginning to feel the need for a legal aid centre. These women knew nothing about their rights. Even I didn't, for that matter. We had no idea about the various government welfare schemes. Perhaps we were entitled to some of them. Another idea I had been toying with was of having a kitchen garden. The women didn't know anything about nutrition. They had to be shown various vegetables and how to cook them. However, our biggest need at this point, as I was beginning to suspect, was to unify these women. Getting them to register had been easy but getting them to work together was near impossible.

These were the thoughts buzzing around in my head and confusing me. Sometimes, they even kept me awake at night, which

I couldn't bear — especially not after having waged such a turbulent war to win my precious sleep back.

After battling with this problem for weeks, I finally reached the conclusion that we needed professional help. Solomon and I could not run the centre on our own. Shailaja was of course there, but she just helped me, you know. I had her unconditional support and she would do anything I asked her to, and help me with anything I was doing, but she could not help me plan. And most importantly, she could not tell me where I was going wrong.

I had decided to call a meeting. I think I had scheduled it for a Monday, about two weeks after the Trax had been vandalised. That day, Solomon came with me to the bank because he too had some work. Nandu and Shailaja were already waiting for Solomon and me when we walked into the office. Lucky ran in ahead of us and jumped on to the broad windowsill. In five minutes he was fast asleep. Aaftab walked in just behind us and asked if he could sit in too. Strictly speaking, he was an outsider but he was more than welcome. If I had a peacock throne, I'd have made him sit on it. If I had frankincense, I'd have burned it. If I had musicians, I'd have called for music. But I didn't have any of these things. So I just engineered it such that he got the most comfortable chair; nudging Solomon out of the way and instantly bringing on that smile that I had gotten so used to by now that I had stopped paying any attention to it.

Nandu stood up as soon as Solomon entered and reached down to touch his feet. Solomon bent down and pulled him up before hugging him. This was a ritual with the two of them. Even if they had met the day before and had spent hours together, Nandu would still touch Solomon's feet the next day and Solomon would still hug him as though he hadn't seen him for years. It really mystified me.

'Why do you that each time you meet?' The question that had been on my mind was out before I could decide whether it was 'proper' or not.

Nandu looked a little uneasy as he replied, 'Because I've known him all my life and I love him.' And then he added, 'You know that my father was very close to him.' This set off a trail in my head, like a thread unraveling. Parameshwaran, the man who had never left Kunnathur had been Narayanankutty's best friend.

'Did Narayanankutty keep in touch with your father after he was released from jail?' The question came as if from a great distance and I expected the answer to be in the negative. I expected Nandu to shake his head and say that my uncle had not written to anybody. But that didn't happen.

A dull red colour stained Nandu's face. He looked down at his feet and didn't say anything. It was Solomon who answered. 'Yes he did.'

I stared at him.

'Is he still alive? Do you know if my uncle still alive?'

'Yes, he is.'

'Does he still write to you ?'

'We... keep in ... touch.'

'Why didn't you tell me? You could have told me, couldn't you? Does he know I'm in Kunnathur? I was yelling now, so loudly that poor Lucky fell off the windowsill. Everybody and everything in the room was silent. The chairs, the table, Shailaja. Everything and everybody. I turned to Shailaja, my best friend, confident that she would mirror my confusion, that she too didn't know anything about all this. If she had known something, she'd have told me. But she too looked away. *Et tu*.

~

*S*olomon got up. He had to go, he said. Saramma wasn't well. Again I was struck by how haggard he looked as he slowly walked out the room. I didn't say anything to him — terribly hurt that he had known something more about Narayanankutty that he hadn't told me. Him, of all the people! He had known how deeply I was involved with Alanghat and my family and yet he hadn't told me.

~

I sat there, lost in these bitter thoughts. The others were leaving the room but I didn't look up and I didn't say anything. That's how the meeting ended — a complete disaster. I sat in the office for some time. Slowly, my anger subsided and with it, the sense of betrayal. It struck me that if Narayanankutty had wanted me to know where he was and if he wanted to get in touch with me, he'd have done so. If he hadn't, it was not Nandu's fault and nor was it Solomon's. If I really considered the situation closely, nothing earth-shattering had happened to make me feel so betrayed. I had merely found out that my uncle had kept in touch with Parameshwaran and Nandu and that he was still alive. There was no need for me to get upset with Nandu or with Solomon over it.

~

I joined the others in the kitchen. Nandu had left. Only Shailaja and Aaftab were left, and of course, Devi and the rest of the gang. Shailaja was mashing cooked jackfruit and Aaftab was grating a coconut — *trying to* grate a coconut. They looked at me carefully, trying to gauge my mood. I grinned at them sheepishly and sat down. Aaftab heaved a gusty sigh of relief and gave me some grated coconut as peace-offering.

I didn't call another meeting immediately because I didn't want to rake up the memory of the last one. Just when I thought that sufficient time had gone by and that it was alright now to meet again, we had some major excitement that made me forget about it altogether.

~

A leading Malayalam newspaper wanted to do a 'piece' on us. They phoned me asking for an appointment. Oh, by the way, by that time Alanghat had acquired a phone connection. The first person to call me had been my father. Nandu had called him secretly and given him the number, the day the phone was installed. He had then phoned me as a sort of surprise. We talked about the centre and I told him about all the developments in the last few weeks. As I chattered away, I realised that I was boasting. *Papa! Look, Papa.* But it was an easy conversation. A natural one. A daughter talking to her father. He didn't say much but I knew he was proud of me. I could sense it, over all those miles of telephone wire.

The next day the people from the newspaper came and interviewed all of us, except Solomon. He couldn't be present as Saramma wasn't feeling well. None of the women went to work that day, and their children didn't go to school. They bunked since they didn't want to pass an opportunity to be photographed for the newspaper. They were all present that morning — all two hundred of them in their best dress, their hair slicked back and a *bhasmakuri* shining on their foreheads. Some of the girls had huge roses, stalk and all, pinned into their plaits. The reporters spent the whole day with us, speaking to the women, Devi, the children, Shailaja, and even Pudukolen. They had dinner with the women and children in the dining hall, photographed everything and left.

Eighteen

*T*hat evening the four of us went to Manuthy to see Saramma. We talked with her for some time, telling her about the day's events. Other than that she looked tired and frail, there seemed nothing seriously wrong with her. Just a bad stomach-upset. She couldn't retain any food, not even soup; but she was cheerful and very happy to see us.

On the way back, Aaftab asked me if I'd like to go with him to the Sri Krishna temple in Guruvayoor the next day, as a sort of celebration for having been interviewed by the press. By the way he said it, I knew he was asking me if I'd like to go there alone with him — just the two of us. It was a date!

The next morning I bathed from head to toe and dressed with extra care. Not just because I was going to the temple at Guruvayoor. I wore a *kasava mundu* - a *mundu* with a *zari* border - and a dark-red silk blouse with paisley motifs in *zari* on the sleeves. After nearly two years, I used *kajal* in my eyes and dabbed some *kumkumum* on my forehead. Feeling a little sheepish, I put flowers in my hair, after which I stared at myself for a long time in the mirror. I couldn't recognise myself. And I knew that Aaftab would not recognise me either. He had never seen me in anything other than jeans and cotton shirts, which I wore against every fashion diktat in Kunnathur. Not in defiance but because I simply couldn't be bothered.

I walked out of the house, to where Aaftab was waiting, scratching Lucky's head. That was the painful thing about Lucky. If he caught you sitting around doing nothing, he would tell you to scratch him. And you just couldn't refuse.

Aaftab looked up as I walked towards him by the way he looked at me, I knew that my efforts in front of the mirror had been worth it. We drove out in silence — *we* were silent, Lucky wasn't. He had begun howling like a wolf. He hated it when I went somewhere, leaving him behind.

I had butterflies in my stomach and I couldn't understand why. Aaftab and I had become friends — I knew him well by now and I was very comfortable with him. Yet, that day, as we next to each other in the Trax, I sensed an unfamiliar quality about him. It was as if I were seeing him for the first time. Something that had been lying dormant within me surfaced and suddenly, I had nothing to hide. There was something between us, as tangible as a third person sitting there. I knew then that this trip would somehow change things between us. Aaftab and I would no longer just be friends. The thought frightened me even as it made me happy. I wanted to be with him, I had no doubt about that. I wanted to be a part of his life — a permanent fixture, like his wristwatch. I wanted to do things for him. Iron his shirt, make his coffee, buy his after-shave. I wanted the right - the *adhikaaram* - to do these things. The *adhikaaram* to worry about him, to get angry with him. In short, I wanted to be married to him. I didn't want that half-an-inch of space to exist between us anymore. Though only half-an-inch, it was capable of turning into a yawning chasm. I was sure of all this; yet, sitting there in the Trax, with the wind blowing in my hair, I was apprehensive. I felt unprotected and vulnerable.

~

*W*e reached Guruvayoor and parked the Trax in the parking lot next to the *satram*. We walked down the road to the *Kezhake Nada* - the east entrance - and booked two rooms in one of the lodges there, right next to the *nada*. The lodge was not much of a place. My room had a bed with sheets stained with *neel*, a towel of dubious cleanliness hanging on a rack and a jug of water on a table. There was a sofa in one corner, with its springs broken. The floor was a depressing, dark-yellow mosaic. I quickly washed my face and did my hair again. Outside, near the shops, I found Aaftab waiting for me. One look at his face told me that he was not too impressed with his room either.

Shops lined the road to the east *nada*, selling all kinds of things
— brass, trinkets, cassettes, flowers, handicrafts, books, saris.
Further down was the *mandapam* where marriages are solemnised
and opposite that was the auditorium, where music and dance
performances were organised.

~

*I*t was only when we reached the *nada* and had entered the
temple that I noticed Aaftab had changed into a *mundu* and *veshti*,
leaving his torso bare, as was the rule in Guruvayoor. He looked
like a Hindu and seemed to know all the sacred spots in the wall
even better than I did. He touched his forehead and the centre of
his chest to the floor, murmured something under his breath and
stepped over the threshold. Nobody could have guessed that he
was not a Hindu. I began to breathe easily again. Non-Hindus
were not allowed inside the temple and I had no desire whatsoever
to find out what would happen if that rule were flouted.

I stole a sideways glance at him as we walked round the
chuttambalam.(a broad walkway around the shrine usually open
to sky, but in Guruvayoor's case, it was covered). The walls of the
shrine were covered with lamps that were lit on special occasions
or when a devotee had a prayer he wanted answered. On that day,
the lamps were lit and they flickered and danced — thousands of
them. In Guruvayoor, each day is Diwali. Aaftab was still
murmuring and I wondered how he knew so much about temple

worship. I got the feeling that he would be just as comfortable in a church or a mosque; or in a monastery in Tibet; or even in some cult temple.

I moved closer to him to try and figure out what he was murmuring, but I couldn't. There was a long queue of people waiting to move in, and my heart sank when I saw it. If there's anything I hate, it is standing around and waiting. I saw that the queue was inching along. A fat lady, looking hot and bothered and dressed in a heavy brown sari with a five-inch *zari* border had been standing next to me, with sweat running down her temples. Ten minutes later she was still standing where I had left her, still looking hot and bothered, but now she was completely drenched in sweat. Aaftab and I looked at each other and in silent consent, we decided to stand by the *deepastambham*. It was crowded there too, but I stretched and craned my neck and managed to get a good view of Guruvayoorappan, the deity — a much clearer view than the one I would have got had I stood in the queue and gone inside. If you go inside, the priest will give you only one-hundredth of a fraction of a second to stand in front of the deity; and if he isn't yelling *ndengin, ndengin* - move, move - then the other people around continue to push and jostle. On hot days like this one, both things happen. It is quite a harrowing experience, you know. Not one for the faint-hearted.

Standing by the *deepastambham*, I got the best view I'd ever had. I think I saw what the *vigraham*, the deity, actually looked like for the first time in my life. Usually, by the time I have been

pushed along in the queue and have reached the altar, all I've had
is a strong desire to be some place else.

~

*T*hat day was different. Different despite the fact that there
was a man standing next to me in a green checked shirt. He had a
cloth bag hanging from one shoulder from which oozed some murky
substance that added to the myriad fragrances in the temple. It
was different because I had Aaftab standing behind me, holding
on to my plait so that the crowd would not separate us. I could feel
his breath fanning the nape of neck and it did strange things to me.
Part of me wanted to run like the devil — back to the safety of
Alanghat and Solomon and part of me wanted to stand there forever.

When Green Shirt started saying his prayers, loudly and off-
key, Aaftab gave up. He let go of my plait and walked away,
shaking his head and laughing. He sat on the steps of the *devi*
shrine that was closed for worship, and watched the family of
rabbits who lived under one of the massive unused *urlis* that was
kept nearby. I stood there alone, unsure of what to do — too proud
to follow Aaftab and yet, not really wanting to stand there. After
a decent gap of about five minutes, I joined him, pretending to be
satisfied with the *darshanam* I had got.

We decided to stay for the *sheeveli* and the *Krishnattamkali*.
The *Krishnattamkali* is a dance form, a bit like Kathakali, which
depicts the life of Krishna. It goes on for eleven days, until Krishna's

Swargaarohanam, which is enacted on the eleventh day. The performance however doesn't stop at the *Swargaarohanam*, which is the depiction of Krishna's death. It continues into the next day with his rebirth. It has been a part of the rituals of the temple for ages and ages. In fact, it is never performed on stage or on television. If you want to see it, you have to go to the temple and sit on the floor, amidst the rich odour of elephant-dung and watch it. There has been no modernisation of the art form at all, which I think is a good thing. Even the clothes look the same — handed down century after century. The performance starts at about nine in the evening and ends at two in the morning, just before the *vaagachath*, the first *puja* of the day.

Each of us had a *dosa* roasted in *ghee* at one of the hotels, after which we went back into the temple through the *Padinjaar Nada* - the west *nada*. There was an even seedier lodge than ours near the west *nada*, which had its tariff list hanging outside. Single cot, single room, room with fan, deluxe, super deluxe. Aaftab said that the room was "super deluxe" if it had a door you could close. He said it so seriously that I wondered if he had ever stayed there. During peak seasons, the temple was so crowded that one had to take whatever accommodation one found and be thankful for it.

Just opposite was the temple tank. During the thirties, people were allowed to take a dip in it. The crowds were smaller then. There was a big sign outside the tank — a list of do-nots; do not urinate in the water, do not spit in the water, do not use oil before taking a dip... . All common sense, and yet we have to be told these things! If we aren't told, we will go ahead and do all of them — and more, if we can think of anything more.

The *sheeveli* was late by an hour that day. By the time the elephants had lined up and the men with lamps and the *panch-vaadyam* musicians had taken their positions, it was nearly ten-thirty. A *Nambutiri* came out with the *vigraham* and climbed onto the back of the biggest elephant. Watching him do that, one would have thought that climbing onto the back of an elephant was the simplest thing in the world. It isn't, take it from me. I have tried doing it and was nearly killed in the process. Behind him, boys climbed onto the two smaller elephants, carrying peacock-feather fans and plumes. The *panch-vaadyam* began, the *chenda* players rolled their heads as their drums reverberated in the limited confines of the *chuttambalam*.

The lamp-holders started walking, carrying lamps hanging from rods in the crook of their arm. Right in the centre, the biggest elephant carrying the *vigraham*, began to move regally down the *chuttambalam*, flanked by the two other elephants. And so, Guruvayurappan got his daily dose of fresh air. He was taken round his temple thrice, after which it was back to the same old petitions and demands. A group of people walked behind the elephants, singing *Hare Krishna, Hare Krishna, Hare Krishna, Hare Hare* to the rhythm of a thousand *manjiras*. I saw a determined old lady, yelling the loudest and banging the *manjira* with all her strength, hitting her fingers most of the time.

Right above, high on the roof, was a white cat illuminated by the stars, washing her face and watching confusion below. The rabbits under the *urli*, the cat on the roof, the elephants in the *sheeveli* and the old woman with the *manjira* — all God's creatures and all divine.

We settled down to watch the *Krishnattamkali* after that. That day's episode was the *Udhava Geeta*. Both of us didn't understand a word but we watched anyway. It felt nice to sit next to Aaftab. It didn't strike me until much later how incongruous the entire scene was, how unromantic in the urban sense of the word. There was no candlelight and no roses. Just elephant-dung and *Krishnattamkali*. But that night, I could feel the magic. It was there in Aaftab's eyes and I was bewitched. I sat there, happy as I could be, giggling like a schoolgirl and completely oblivious of the time until the performance suddenly finished, breaking the spell and bringing me back to earth with a thud.

~

I leapt out of bed at four in the morning, after barely two hours of sleep, to the sound of persistent knocking on my door. I opened it to find Aaftab, all bathed and ready to leave. He looked radiantly fresh in his white *kurta-pyjama,,* with his hair wet and subdued for a change. I stared at him, dazed, through hair that was falling all over my face — yesterday's flowers still hanging by a pin. Why did he want to leave at four in the morning? It was pitch dark outside!

But we left anyway, after having a cup of coffee in one of the hotels. Nice coffee — like *Pattamaar inte kaapi*, the coffee made by *Pattamaar*, non-Malayali Brahmins. For Nayar*s*, coffee couldn't get better than that! *Enda aayaalum, Pattamaar kaapi nanai indaakam*! Whatever it is, *Pattamaar* make good coffee!

Poor Aaftab kept falling asleep at the wheel. After a while, I took over and he curled up and went to sleep. I drove for some time in silence and then, right in the middle of nowhere, the engine stopped. Just like that, without a warning. Aaftab had to get out of the Trax and push it for quite a distance before the engine woke up again. There seemed to have been a problem with some wire. We drove along for some time, enjoying the cool *pulercha* - daybreak-breeze. The exercise seemed to have done him some good because he sat up and took some interest in our surroundings. Not much — s*ome*! It was many days later, while we were having one of our after-dinner-chats on the telephone that he told me why we had left so suddenly.

His room had been full of mosquitoes and it did not have a ceiling-fan — not a fan that worked, anyway. The night had been unbearable, and just when he was dropping off out of sheer exhaustion, the handicrafts shop below his room started playing *Harinama kirthans* loud enough to wake up Jesus Christ in Trichur, leave alone Guruvayurappan next door. It seemed particularly loud to Aaftab. Every quaver in the warped cassette had been deafening. Then he discovered why. One of the loudspeakers was attached to his window, facing inwards, into the room. With that, he admitted defeat and came to my room to wake me up, deciding that there was no need for me to sleep either.

Just as we were reaching Manuthy, the Trax stopped again. Aaftab turned to me and said, 'Your turn to push.' I climbed out of the Trax, hitched my *kasava mundu* up, tucked it in and started pushing. It *was* my turn.

Nineteen

Visu

*B*ack at Alanghat, I went straight to my room and crawled into bed, waking up only at lunchtime. The newspaper carried our article that day, with a big photograph of the women standing in front of Alanghat. There was a small photograph of me too, with my name under it. Aaftab went to Cheriathur to have the page enlarged and framed. He hung it up in our office and it still hangs there — our first taste of fame.

The article generated a lot of interest all over Kerala, and we began receiving donations in cash and in kind from several people. I think we were able to retain most of the people as regular donors through the years because right from the start we were very prompt in replying to all the letters, with either more information or a letter of appreciation. All the same, if I'd known the havoc that article was going to create, I'd never have agreed to the interview.

~

*S*aramma took a turn for the worse and Solomon didn't come to the centre for three day, so we would all go to his house in the evening to see her. She was losing weight at an alarming rate and couldn't retain any food even now. She had also developed a severe stabbing pain in the stomach. Dr. Krishnankutty was treating her but the medication made her feel better only for a brief spell. Solomon was beginning to look very anxious and nervous. He seemed to have great faith in Aaftab and Aaftab, in turn, seemed to know just what to say to reassure him. One would never have guessed, looking at all of us together, that we had known him only for a few weeks. There was something very measured about him. Very balanced. He was not at all like Vivek — in fact, they were poles apart. The way I felt towards him was nowhere close to the way I had felt towards Vivek. Vivek had been heady and intoxicating, like the fragrance of opium. Aaftab didn't intoxicate me — he just made me feel satisfied. Complete. I felt, even way back then, that I had known him all my life. I loved to see him potter about the place; entering records in the register, typing letters, making tea. I liked to sit next to him and do nothing. Sometimes we'd spend our evenings in the front porch of Alanghat, bored to tears, dying for some entertainment — any kind of entertainment! We had heard all our cassettes from start to finish about a thousand times each. We had read all our books. We had driven just about everywhere. Now there was nothing left to do. So we'd sit in the

212

porch and pick fights with each other, too bored to even do that properly. I really wasn't *bored* - bored, you know. I was *happy* - bored. And I knew that he was too, which made me even *happier-* bored.

Initially, I thought I had to feel for him the same way as I did for Vivek — only then would my feelings for him fall under the 'love' category. So I was quite disappointed when I felt differently. But as I got closer to Aaftab, I began to realise that my feelings for him were not half-baked and lukewarm. I knew in time that it was okay to feel differently — after all these were two different people, two different chapters in my life; one closed forever and the other just unfolding. I refuse to say that the way I felt towards him was "good in its own way" because I don't like the phrase, *in its own way.* Doesn't it sound like a consolation prize? *Good but not good enough — you're only good in your own way. You're okay in your own league — just see to it that you stay there!* No, my feelings for Aaftab were not *good in their own way.* They were - and still are - the best that I am capable of. Wholesome, tender and deep. He brings out all that is the gentlest and the finest in me and I love him with all my heart.

~

*L*ook where I have wandered. At this rate, I'll never finish my story! It rained quite heavily for the next three days. I was buying some rice from Nandu's shop on what seemed to be a nice dry day when suddenly it began to pour, as if something in the sky had given way. The road in front of the shop turned into a river in no time and I had to wade to the Trax in water that reached my calves. That night, while Devi and Parameshwari slept, and Lucky and I sat in the porch watching the lightning, we saw the *padipera* door open and Aaftab come in. He ran up to the porch when he saw us sitting there. Saramma was seriously ill, he said and Solomon had taken her to Trichur. He had phoned Aaftab, asking him to get the Trax and reach the nursing-home where she had been admitted. Within five minutes he had taken the Trax and was gone. I sat there for a long time, now oblivious to the lightening and the rain. I thought about Saramma, worrying about what the next few days would have in store for us and waiting for Aaftab to phone.

The next morning I awoke early and took a bus to Trichur, leaving Lucky behind. Aaftab had phoned at three in the morning to say the doctors suspected cancer of the intestines and Saramma was to be operated upon immediately. I spent the entire day with Solomon and Aaftab in the hospital and then took the evening bus back. By the time I reached Alanghat, it was dark. Devi had left the porch light on. As I was entering the house, I saw something black lying near the mango tree. I walked up to it, thinking that one of the children had left something there.

When I reached there, I found that it was Lucky. He was lying there with his stomach ripped open and he was drenched. I knelt down beside him, staring at the horrible sight. I called out to Devi, unable to keep the hysteria out of my voice. Devi came running out, alarmed. When she saw me sitting there holding Lucky — his gut spilling out into my hands, she screamed. She started jabbering incoherently. *He had been with her all the time…aiyooo, how did this happen…he had been with her all this time…aiyo, she had just gone to bathe…not even half an hour ago…even half an hour was not up…then she was feeding the baby…she had just started feeding the baby…just now. Aiyo. Aiyo. Aiyo. Aiyo… .*

~

*I*t was then that I felt him lick me. I felt it again. He was still alive! I grabbed Devi's upper cloth and bound him up. I looked around for the Trax. *No Trax!* I shouted to Devi to get a basket. We lifted him into it and I started walking as fast as I could to Dr. Krishnankutty's house. By the time I reached the *padipera*, it was raining buckets again. Finally, after what seemed like hours, I reached Krishnankutty's house and rang the doorbell, praying that he would be home and that he wouldn't refuse to treat Lucky. He was and he didn't. We spent two hours disinfecting and stitching up Lucky. By this time, I was thinking fairly clearly. I knew that this was the work of Shankaran Nayar and I was livid.

I sat up with Lucky the entire night. In the morning, his condition was worse. Dr. Krishnankutty thought he had contracted pneumonia. He had also lost a lot of blood. The angry knot in my stomach hadn't loosened. In fact, it had grown tighter. No Muthote Shankaran Nayar was going to decide whether Lucky was going

215

to live or die! I phoned Hari and asked him to bring his car. Hari was the person who had driven me to Alanghat on my first day in Kunnathur. I paced the room as I waited for him. Once Hari arrived, I pushed him out of the way and placed Lucky in the back seat and drove out of there like a bat out of hell.

The veterinary hospital in Trichur was a dilapidated structure. The attendant took one look at Lucky and shook his head. I slammed the door on his face, narrowly missing it and drove to Coimbatore. There was no point in trying Palakkad. It couldn't have been any better than Trichur. I had just one thought - just one - in my head.

I found the veterinary hospital and Lucky was admitted. I sat next to him in a long bare room while they re-dressed his wound. Krishnankutty had been right — Lucky did have pneumonia. I sat there wondering over and over again what the little dog had done to deserve this. When I heard Lucky whimper, the anger within me raged as if somebody had sprinkled kerosene over it. I sprang up and stormed out of the place and drove all the way back to Kunnathur, making that ancient chariot of a car, with its red and green disco lights, do things it had never done in its entire life.

I stopped outside the *panchayat* office, the wheels screeching as I slammed the brakes. Shankaran Nayar wasn't there. Reversing straight into the potted plants that lined the driveway and breaking as many as I could, I drove to Shankaran Nayar's house. Not bothering to ring the bell, I stormed into his sitting room with Hari's crowbar in my hand. He was sitting there and talking to V.K.Menon. As soon as he saw me, he got up to say something. I pushed him back and slapped him hard. Twice, on either cheek.

'What have I ever done to you, you bastard. What? Tell me...what have I ever done to you?' I was roaring and I could feel the blood rushing to my face.

'You want to be Panchaayat President, is that it? Is that it? So be, damn it! Who the hell is stopping you?' I whirled around the room like a tornado, upsetting chairs and smashing a grotesque vase of bright pink plastic flowers that sat on top of the TV.

By now his wife, two sons and their maid were cowering behind the door. His wife was holding on to her two sons, restraining them from coming out and joining the fray. From the corner of my eye, I saw a smug photograph of Shankaran Nayar in the showcase. I tightened my grip on Hari's crowbar, lifted it up and smashed it down on the showcase. The photograph toppled over and fell down. I stepped on it and ground my heel into his nose. There was a glass-topped cane table there — I smashed that too.

V.K. Menon came towards me to try and stop me. He was a thin, scrawny, pip-squeak of a man. 'Don't touch me,' I snarled, waving the crowbar at him.

'Get out of the way, you little shit'. I turned towards Shankaran Nayar and gasped, 'If anything happens to Lucky - if Lucky dies - I'll stone you out of this village.' At the word "stone", I lifted the crowbar and hit the TV. Nothing happened but the sound seemed to echo in the silent room. With that I stormed out, still quivering in anger.

But I hadn't finished. Shankaran Nayar's red Maruti was parked in the porch. I lifted the crowbar once again and brought it down with all my might, making sure that this time something happened. The windshield shattered, glass flying all over the place. Tit for tat.

Only then did I drive out of there, my anger on the wane. I drove all the way back to Coimbatore. Lucky was sleeping. I sat next to him, leaned my head against the wall and after a while, dozed off into an uncomfortable sleep.

~

Genes are such funny things. Raman Nayar really tormented me until I figured out how to control him. I am quite proud to say that I never lost my temper so completely ever again. It helps to repeat *I will not lose my temper* over and over again when you feel it coming. I even made a little song out of it.

Twenty

I heard footsteps and opened my eyes to find Aaftab sitting on his haunches in front of me. He had a three-day stubble on his face and his eyes looked tired and drawn. We looked at each other sympathetically, our fingers interlinked. He had bad news for me. Saramma's condition was beyond hope. The doctor's had opened her up only to find her riddled with malignant tumours. So they had just stitched her up again and given her not more than a day to live. They said it was a sort of galloping cancer. He offered to sit with Lucky so that I could go to Trichur and spend some time with Saramma. I bent over Lucky. He was sleeping but he had a raging temperature. I walked to the car and climbed in to again drive back to Trichur. It was not yet dawn and the streets were deserted.

When I reached the hospital, Saramma was alone in the room. I sat on the bed next to her and looked down at her pale, tired face, tears filling my eyes. She saw the tears and reached out, taking my hand in hers and held it. We sat like that for a long time. Then she whispered to me to tell the doctors to remove the tubes from her hand. I stared at her, hesitating to comply with her request.

She looked at me and said, 'I am dying, *koche*. I don't need these tubes.'

'You aren't going to die, Saramma,' I said. 'Something will happen and you'll get better.'

'Nothing will happen. My time has come and I'm ready to go. Don't stop me, *koche*. Don't hold me back.'

I stared at her helplessly, tears welling up again.

'Can you comb my hair for me?'

I picked up a comb from the table with a mirror and started running it as gently as I could through her thin, grey hair.

She started talking about her childhood in Etumannur. They had lived in a small house. It had one long room and one small room and a kitchen. That was all. Her entire family, eleven of them, lived there. Nine children and her parents. Her father had been a pastor. Her best friend had been a girl called Shiny. She broke off and asked me to remove her hospital gown and dress her in one of her own nighties. I hesitated again but this time only for a fraction of a second. I sponged her with a wet towel and buttoned her up in a fresh robe with a floral print.

When she started talking again, it was about a dream she had had the previous night. She said an angel had visited her. She had seen him standing their at the foot of her bed and the light had dazzled her. She had woken up then and had continued to see the dazzling light at the foot of her bed. That is why she had sent Solomon to fetch the priest. She ran her tongue over her dry lips. I picked up a glass of water and spooned some warm water into her mouth. I wondered whether she should be talking so much. But then again, as she said, she was dying. If she felt like speaking, let her. However, she stopped talking after drinking the water and lay back against the pillow, her forehead creased into furrows of pain. I put a hand on her forehead and smoothed out the lines and she closed her eyes.

The door opened and Solomon came in. Behind him was a priest, the doctor and a nurse. Solomon looked at me, walked over to a chair in the corner of the room and sat down. There was a stillness about him, as if he was drawing all his energy inwards. He was praying. Saramma slipped into unconsciousness a short while later. And then she was dead.

~

*T*he funeral was the next day, at the Pentecost Church in Manuthy. Solomon sat in silence throughout the service. Dignified in his grief but alone, as though he had nobody left. There was a stream of visitors, from the church to their small house in Manuthy and so I was busy in the kitchen, making and serving tea the entire day. I was bone-tired by then. If I stood still I swayed, so I had to keep moving about. All I wanted to do was to go back to Alanghat and sleep. But I couldn't do that; I couldn't leave Solomon alone. And there in Coimbatore, what was happening to Aaftab and Lucky?

I was relieved when I saw Nandu walking in with someone behind him. Perhaps I could leave now that Nandu was here. But I was in for a shock. The man behind Nandu was a policeman and he was there to arrest me for attacking Shankaran Nayar and smashing up his house in the presence of five witnesses.

As I got into his car and was driven off, I could see Solomon standing there; his face haggard, his shoulders drooping and a devastated look in his eyes. He was still standing like that when I turned to look at him one last time. That look never really left him, you know. It stayed with him even when he smiled. It was as if something inside him had died that day. It had put up a valiant battle all this time but had finally accepted defeat.

Twenty One

I spent *Visu* in jail. *Visu* falls on the first of the month of *Medam*, on the fourteenth of April and marks the Malayali New Year. I had planned to have *Visu Kani* for all the women in the centre. I had even taken out the best *urli* Alanghat had and asked Devi to polish it. That's how *Visu* is celebrated, you know. We wake up at four thirty in the morning and the first thing we see is the *urli* placed in front of a lamp. The *urli* is filled with jackfruit, bananas, coconuts, rice, a new *mundu*, gold, a yellow cucumber, the yellow flowers of the *konda* tree, betel leaves and nuts and a small mirror known as the *kani*. Actually, we are supposed to walk with our eyes closed and seat ourselves in front of the *urli*. Then we wash our eyes with a little water and open them so that the first thing we see on *Visu* day is the *kani*. It is an unspoken prayer for prosperity and happiness - *aishwaryam* - for the whole year round.

~

*N*ow all that was forgotten. Saramma was dead. For all I knew, perhaps Lucky was too. And I was in jail. The policeman had asked me why I had smashed up Shankaran Nayar's house and I had told him the whole story. He had listened to the whole thing quite sympathetically but he asked me a question for which I had absolutely no answer. 'Where is the proof?' There was no proof. I had no proof at all. I just *knew* that it was Shankaran Nayar whose men had smashed my Trax and ripped Lucky's stomach.

I sat in that miserable cell all night, looking at the sky through a tiny little hole in the wall, which was all I had for a window. I could see two stars through the hole and on that night, those two stars became the emissaries of the world outside. The stars and I stayed up together, waiting for the crack of dawn.

Strangely though, that morning I had the best *Visu kani* I have ever had. Solomon came to see me at four-thirty in the morning. The small police station was dark and quiet. The constable on duty was dozing. Only I was awake. I saw Solomon enter and we stood looking at each other for long moment. Me, pathetically, through the bars of the cell and him, gravely, from the main door. But I noticed something lurking behind his usual gravity and his personal grief. He was laughing!

Slowly, I relaxed. Everything was going to be all right. I didn't know how, but I wasn't worried anymore. If Solomon could come to the police station at four-thirty in the morning and laugh, then everything must be all right.

The constable opened the cell and allowed Solomon to sit next to me. He sat quietly with me for a few minutes with his hand on my head, smoothing my hair. Just before leaving he turned around and said, this time failing miserably to conceal a smile, 'Aaftab is arranging your bail. I think you'll be out of here by tomorrow.' Reassured, I curled up on the bare plank that was my bed and fell asleep.

They offered me some *kanji* the next morning, which I refused. I felt that if I ate it I would really become a criminal. It had been a difficult thing to do because I was actually starving. I was also dog-tired and I hadn't brushed my teeth for three days, ever since I had found Lucky lying with his stomach ripped open under the mango tree. I was also running a fever of 103 degrees, which I didn't know at that time. Aaftab came with a lawyer from Trichur and I was released from jail at 12.30 the same afternoon.

I came out to find all the women from the centre standing outside the police station. They had held a *jatha* right down the main road of Kunnathur, complete with banners and placards, demanding that I be released immediately. I stood there embarrassed and uncomfortable with all this attention. But the women had only just begun. They started shouting slogans and surged forward as soon as they saw me, surrounding me completely. One of them even had a garland of marigolds which she threw around my neck. Worse still, somebody was taking photographs. I found myself being propelled towards the Trax. In all the confusion, I recognised the journalist who had interviewed me the last time and nodded a greeting to him. He asked me what my next move was going to be. That bewildered me. *Move?* I hadn't been making any *moves*! I turned around to tell him that, when Aaftab caught me by the elbow and dumped me unceremoniously into the back seat, got in himself and drove off.

I nearly collapsed with relief once I was back at cool and quiet Alanghat. But only nearly. I couldn't afford the luxury just yet, Aaftab informed me. I had one more thing to do — the hardest thing of all. I had to go to Shankaran Nayar's house and apologise for smashing it up and pay for the damages. According to my father, that was the only way out.

My father! My father knew I had been arrested! I stared at Aaftab, absolutely horrified as the ramifications of that statement slowly sank into my tired brain. He returned my stare with an unsympathetic one of his own and spoke flatly. How did I suppose I was given bail? Had I given it a thought? Solomon had paid and my father was sending the money to reimburse him. That's how I had been released.

I sat back in my chair and looked out of the window, digesting the news — or at least, trying to. A *konda* tree was in full bloom just outside. It's bright yellow flowers and light green leaves dappled by the sunlight and shade were swaying in the warm summer breeze; nodding their heads, reassuring me kindly and sympathetically. I turned back to Aaftab. There was no kindliness and sympathy there. His eyes had a "serves you right, you crazy cow" look. So I gathered my last ounce of strength and courage and drove off to Shankaran Nayar's house, with Aaftab sitting next to me for moral support.

I parked the Trax outside the gate and climbed out declining Aaftab's offer to accompany me. I didn't want an audience. I walked through the open gate, shuffling and dragging my feet a little. I couldn't believe I was doing this. I was actually going to apologise to Muthote Shankaran Nayar for allowing him to rip apart my dog and smash the windscreen of my Trax!

This time I rang the doorbell. It had a horrible sound but then what else can one expect in a purple coloured house? Shankaran Nayar's wife opened the door. I stared at her, my mouth refusing to open. She indicated a chair and scurried out of the room. He made me wait for a long time. Deliberately. Then he walked in and without looking at me, sat down in his armchair. He arranged his *mundu*, took his glasses out of their case and put them on. Then he called out to his wife to bring him his tea. She brought one cup of tea and put it down on the small table next to him. All this while, I was sitting in one of the chairs arranged against the wall, being made to feel like a small petitioner.

I took a deep breath and closed my mind to everything. I heard him put down his cup and say, 'Yes, what do you want?' I muttered my lines and gave him the cheque. He stared at me for an instant. I stared back, the atmosphere in the room thick with hostility. He took the cheque and dismissed me with a movement of his head. I left the room and walked back to the Trax.

But the matter didn't end there because that journalist had found the man who had smashed my Trax and ripped Lucky apart; and the man had confessed to committing both crimes on Shankaran Nayar's instruction and on the payment of a considerable fee. The same journalist had also met Devi, without my knowledge, and she had told him about Shankaran Nayar's visit to Alanghat on that infamous Sunday, somewhere around *Shivarathri*.

The newspaper carried the whole story the next day, complete with photographs of Shankaran Nayar. Needless to say, I got all the sympathy. Letters of support poured in at Alanghat and to the newspaper's offices, from all over Kerala — letters of reassurance and support, urging me to continue the work I was doing and "not buckle under demonic forces," as one letter put it.

~

*S*o, my apology was lost in the wind and the battle lines, vague and imaginary until then, were firmly marked and drawn between Shankaran Nayar and me.

Twenty Two

*B*ack at Alanghat after the apology, I had a bath and ate some food. By that time, my fever was raging and I was burning inside, my lips dry and my eyes unnaturally bright. I tossed and turned in bed, looking for a cool spot on my pillow but not finding one. Krishnankutty was called in and after a check-up, he declared that I needed complete rest and was not to get out of bed for the next one week.

I lay in bed, worried about Lucky. I fretted for so long, not sleeping and not eating that poor Aaftab finally got into the Trax and drove to Coimbatore. Lucky was much better a week after his harrowing experience and the vet said he could be taken home, though he still needed of rest and medication. So Lucky came home to a hero's welcome, less than half his size, his eyes huge and vulnerable in his thin face.

Two days later Aaftab returned to Bombay taking the salt out of my life. The day he left, I took a turn for the worse, my fever suddenly shooting up again and forcing me to throw up everything I ate. Solomon was at my side all through, going to Nandu's place only to bathe and sleep. After about a week, when the fever hadn't subsided, he called a doctor from Trichur and my medicines were changed. Only then did I get better.

The two weeks that I spent recuperating is a time that I will remember and cherish all my life. And more, if that is possible. Solomon would sit in the easy chair by the side of my bed, Lucky would be sleeping on some cushions at his feet and the three of us would talk about so many things.

Solomon was a walking encyclopedia. There was nothing in this world that he didn't know something about or didn't have a book about. Over the last year or so I had slipped into the habit of "referring to Solomon" for any problem I had — arithmetic, an event in history, politics, philosophy... or even with spelling.

One evening, I was sitting up in bed and Solomon was dozing in the armchair. That actually, was quite an unusual sight. He usually sat staring out of the window, lost in some unhappy thought, with a defeated look in his sad eyes. Since Saramma's death, he had grown even quieter - if that was possible - spending more and more time by himself, and it troubled me quite a bit. But I didn't feel comfortable asking him because that was a part of him that was very private. I was relieved to see him dozing that day. I felt reassured. As if everything was okay. I had been thinking about my visit to the *Shiva Kshetram* on the morning of *Shivarathri*. All right, I'll be honest. I had been thinking about Aaftab, wondering why he hadn't called or written. He had phoned just once, as soon as he reached and had spoken to Solomon. After that, there had been no news. I spent a lot of time secretly thinking about him and praying for a letter or a phone call. That morning too, I had been brooding and trying to force myself to think about something else. And so I began pondering over this Shiva fixation that I had.

Was I a devotee of Shiva? How could I be a devotee when I didn't believe in the existence of God? I didn't believe that there was a God sitting in eternal meditation on the top of a mountain; though I have to admit that once when I saw a documentary on Mount Kailash, I felt it was quite possible that Shiva was sitting there, right on the top. But that is because the place seemed like that — silent and eternal. It made one feel that way because we ourselves are so transient, so evanescent. Our small minds cannot contain a concept that is Formless and Timeless. Eternity, for most of us, is a good name for a bottle of perfume or for a song about undying love and fidelity.

So who was Shiva? Was he actually watching over me? I tried to extricate from my mind the idea that there was an omniscient, omnipresent One watching over me, always standing by, ready to rescue me. Suppose there was nobody. Suppose there was just me and my actions, which in turn, lead to more actions. The awesome responsibility implied by the thought frightened me and I quickly put Shiva back in position. But the idea had already taken root.

Was faith actually fear in disguise? Was there no Shiva? Was there no God? Was I alone in this mess?

I shook Solomon awake. Was I in this fearsome place alone? He blinked and after a second closed his eyes again. I thought he had gone back to sleep but he hadn't. He opened them again and asked for some tea. I pushed away the pillow I had on my knees in exasperation. Here I was struggling on the brink of a great spiritual breakthrough and all he could think of was *tea*!

He slowly sipped at his tea and took his time answering me. 'There is God.' He said it categorically, dispelling some of my agitation. But his next line mystified me completely. 'It is you that is a figment of your own imagination'. He didn't elaborate on that. Perhaps he knew that I wouldn't understand a word. Shiva, he said, veering off to the other part of my question, was the Great God seated on Mount Kailash. Mount Kailash is the centre of the Universe, just as a circle has a centre. But because here we are dealing with infinitude, the centre is everywhere and the circumference is nowhere. Truth, wisdom and illumination emanate from him. Since we all yearn for these things, since we are constantly seeking deliverance from loneliness, sorrow and conflict, we yearn for Him. It would amount to the same thing if we yearned for truth, wisdom and illumination but we don't do that. We tend to believe that Shiva will lead us into Light, instead of the other way around. The Light is contained in Shiva. It does not contain Shiva. Once I reach Shiva, I will have no use for the Light because I would have merged with the Source. Solomon said it was like

232

using a torch only until the electricity was restored. Once there is electricity, will I continue to use the torch? The answer to that was obviously a dutiful shake of the head and so I shook mine. But there had been a time, once, when I had continued to use my torch, you know, for quite some time after the electricity had been restored. I hadn't realised that it was there.

Shiva, according to mythology, has three eyes. The ordinary two are for perceiving the phenomenal world — the sun, the moon, space, earth — the world as we see it. The third eye is spiritual and intuitive. It suggests transcendental knowledge and is characteristic of Godhood. Apparently, we humans can have access to Godhood too. Having descended from divinity, man has the possibility of a latent Godhood in him and it can be reached through stillness of the mind and the complete acceptance of the present. If you can do that, you reach knowledge and intuition. Truth is self-explained in intuition and has to be experienced. It cannot be confined to a definition or to an image brought about by words, like the word "night".

Solomon stopped here and got up to switch on the light and shut the window. It was getting dark and soon it would be night. He settled down in his chair again, looking at Lucky to check if he was comfortable. I still carry that snapshot with me, deep in my heart — the three of us sitting there, snug and comfortable in our brightly lit room, with dusk falling rapidly outside. The yellow light from the bulb hanging in its old-fashioned shade up above, shone on Solomon's silvery hair, reflected on Lucky's shiny black coat, caught the brightness of my red blanket and enveloped all of us in it's mellow, happy warmth.

Solomon turned towards me and started to speak again, his dry, papery whisper sounding clear and strong in the silence of our little world. *Rudra* is another name given to Shiva, he said. It is the characterization of Shiva as *Rudra* that many people believe in. R*udra*, Solomon said, is the one who torments and makes one weep, but at the same time bestows relief and benediction. (In that respect, what was written in my *ola* in the *nadi shastra* is true for all mankind. I wasn't special. I hadn't been singled out. What was true for me was true for all of humanity.).

But why does He want to do that, I asked? Why does He want to torment us and make us weep and then bestow relief and benediction? Why can't He leave us all alone and let us get on with it as best as we can? Solomon's answer was typical of Solomon. 'Who is this He you keep talking about? Aaftab?'

'No. Shiva.'

'Who is Shiva? Where is he?'

'I don't know.'

'He's inside you.'

'He is?'

'He is your valley of clouds.'

'Who? Aaftab?'

'No. Shiva.'

'What?'

'Yes.'

234

Silence.

'*Manas il aayiyo?*' Have you understood?

'*Endhe?*' What?

'*Endhe engilim.*' Anything.

'Uh-uh.'

~

*T*hat night they started beating drums in the temple across the river where my *devi* was. The *Manapulikaavu Vela* - the temple festival - had begun. I lay in bed and listened to the drums as they picked up tempo, slowed down and quickened again. Waiting to fall asleep, I lay thinking about all kinds of things. Mostly about Aaftab. I hadn't heard from him ever since he had left Kunnathur. What was he doing in Bombay? Why hadn't he called? Had he forgotten?

Maybe he didn't want to call. That was one way of telling me that it wouldn't work. Maybe I should keep quiet too and pretend it was just an interlude — a holiday romance. But I didn't want to leave it at that. I wanted to be told nicely and decently. And if he didn't want to be nice and decent on his own, I would make him. I took out my address book and walked to the phone, the drums pounding in rhythm with my heart. How stupid! Nervous about calling Aaftab! When he was here, we would talk to each other every night, don't you remember?

That was when he was here. Things were different then.

What was different? Nothing was different!

The phone at the other end rang. Once. Twice. Thrice. Four times. I felt sick with apprehension. A lady finally answered. I lost my nerve and hung up. Who was she?

I stood by the phone for a long time, the mosquitoes feasting on my bare ankles. When the blood had stopped rushing to my ears, I picked up the receiver and dialed again. This time I took a deep breath and resolved that I would speak no matter who answered the phone. When I heard the receiver being picked up at the other end, I shut my eyes and swallowed hard. But I needn't have bothered. It was Aaftab this time, and he recognized my voice. We chatted for some time about Kunnathur, the centre, my health, Lucky's health, Solomon's health... .

Okay, I admit I chickened out. I couldn't ask him to be a gentleman. My tongue stuck to the roof of my mouth at the very thought of asking such a direct question. There was no change in his manner, if that was any consolation. He seemed as friendly and open as before. Perhaps he was like that with everybody. Maybe that's just his way. Something inside me turned ice-cold and switched off. Suddenly I wanted to hang up. I didn't want to hear what he was saying. It was no concern of mine. Why was he talking so much anyway? I had called out of sheer politeness — a courtesy call. Nothing more.

I went back to bed and lay down with my eyes closed, forcing myself to listen to the drums. To count the *taal*. To concentrate. To breathe. I lay like that, rigid and unmoving, with a sinking feeling in the pit of my stomach. Was it going to start all over again? Had I learnt nothing from the past? No! *Please God, no*!

I don't know when I fell asleep — I just dropped off. But I slept well, as usual. When I woke up, I made a New Year's Resolution. It was May, but never mind. Aaftab was a closed chapter. I would not hope. I would not hope for his return - hope that he would phone - hope that we would get married. I couldn't stop thinking about him. But I would not *hope*.

Twenty Three

'Stillness of the mind', said Solomon, 'cannot be made to happen'. We were walking along the riverbed one evening, at about five. The sun was still bright at that time but not very hot. Not as hot as it had been in the afternoon. It was the second week of May now, and it had been three days since the phone-call to Aaftab. The *puzha* had shrunk to a thin ribbon of water, trickling along the centre of the riverbed. Children held competitions to see who could jump right across her and women spread their laundry on her exposed rocks. By the time they had bathed in the *puzha* and dried themselves, their clothes would be dry too — that is how hot the sun was. It blazed on, blinding and burning us, leaving us exhausted and spent, grateful for the little respite that evening brought.

Solomon was returning to Manuthy the next day, having made

sure that I had recovered completely. We were taking our last walk together that evening, talking about my elusive valley, my valley of the clouds.

'Stillness of the mind cannot be made to happen. No amount of controlling or meditating can bring about true stillness. Making the mind still was different from the mind achieving a stillness of its own. A mind that has been *made* still is in an unnatural state. It has been sedated. One doesn't want a sedated mind, does one?' I shook my head, dumbly. 'What kind of mind does one want?' I dipped my foot in the water and wiggled my toes, not saying anything. 'One wants a mind that is still so that there are no ripples. No conflict. No struggle to achieve, to understand and to improve upon. A complete acceptance of the present state. No conflict between what should be - the ideal state - and what actually is.'

I listened in silence. Conflict. It seemed to me that if there was life, there had to be conflict. One could not escape it. Night and day — there was conflict there. Desire and pain — conflict again. Truth and lies — conflict. Hope and reality — conflict. *Conflict. Conflict. Conflict.* There was conflict wherever I looked! So how could there possibly be a state of No Conflict — a state of complete acceptance?

I lifted my head to look at the sky. It was clear blue, almost white. High above, way overhead, a bird was flying. With each gust of air, it rose higher and higher, till it was a mere speck in the sky. I squinted up, watching it fly till I couldn't see it anymore and then looked down again. From what I understood of the whole thing, which as you can see isn't much, the whole trick in getting rid of conflict is in understanding the mechanism of remembering and forgetting. I had to remember to forget.

Solomon stopped suddenly and turned to look at with me, his eyes burning with a strange kind of intensity, compelling me to look back at him and take what he was giving me. If I could do that, he said, moving his hands forcefully and then bringing them back to his sides, I would be able to make something of this life. If I could do that, after a while I would *forget to remember*. Then there would be no conflict. The sense of urgency - of desperation - with which he said it conveyed itself to me and stirred something within me. It was as if that was his message to me. A message he wanted me to understand.

We stood like that for a split second, in the shade of a coconut tree that grew almost parallel to the river, its fronds hanging directly overhead, the tips trailing in the water. Then the moment passed and we continued walking in silence. I could once again sense the turmoil deep inside him, a turmoil that never left him even for a minute. Then he continued.

As long as the mind is in the grip of memory, we cannot wholly be in the present. We then use the present only as a sort of stepping stone to the future and because of this, our present has no significance of its own. And yet, our present is all that we should understand. Everything else is immaterial. It is our desire to persist in remembering the past that stops us from truly understanding the present because it traps us in-between our yesterday and tomorrow. Our today is the product of our yesterday and it will shape our tomorrow. The past through the present creates the future.

We paused to sit down on the steps of one of the bathing *ghats* that dotted the banks of the *puzha*. Aaftab and I had sat there once, the memory of which brought a smile to my lips. What a fool I was! Not long ago, I was in agony over Vivek and now I was grinning idiotically over Aaftab. Poor deluded fool! I looked up quickly at Solomon to dispel the thought and he took it as an indication that I wanted him to continue.

The past is really just our memory. It does not exist anywhere else. We keep mulling over the past to find answers about our present. If we continue to remember our past and store our memories, instead of wiping the slate clean, how can we live wholly in the present? We can't. And so the mind cannot be free of conflict and it cannot be still. So simple! Q.E.D.

~

*I*t was twilight by the time we walked back, in almost complete silence, each lost in our own thoughts. I began to understand what Solomon meant by "memory". He hadn't been talking about mere facts and events and people. He had been talking about the recesses where we store our pain, our joys and our prejudices. That is the retreat we had to wipe clean. Never let things - debris - collect there, for isn't it true that our pain is caused by the absence of the things that give us joy? If we had no memory of the joy, would we be in pain when that which provides joy is no longer there?

~

I had a lot to live for. The very fact that I was still alive was proof of that. Not just me — every living thing has something to live for. And if there is life, there has to be renewal. Otherwise, why would the *kani konda* blossom in April, every year. Once would have been enough. I had to allow myself to be renewed — by time and by nature. I had to wade in again — and *again*, if need be — until I had conquered my terror of crocodiles and rocks, until I had solved the mystery of the currents and the tides. Perhaps it would take several lives. Perhaps it would take only one.

And Shiva will be there, where I left him. Waiting. Like the ocean waits for the *puzha*. After all, where can the *puzha* go? And how long can it take to return? How does *where* and *how long* compare with *infinitude*? A circle with everywhere as its centre and nowhere as its circumference.

~

I sighed. We had reached the steps that led to Alanghat. Raman Nayar's steps. I ran up, feeling the heat from the stones under my feet and turned to wait for Solomon. He was walking up slowly, his hand gripping the railing till his knuckles showed white. He looked old and frail. This was not just grief over Saramma's death — it was something else.

~

*W*ith that evening's conversation tumbling about in my head, like clothes in a washing machine — *remember to forget, forget to remember* — I fell asleep only to suddenly wake up at midnight and find the whole room bathed in moonlight. *Velutha* vaave. Pournami. It was a full-moon night.

As always, the full moon drew me out into the back porch. To my *puzha*. There was a gentle breeze blowing in, wafting the fragrance of the *pavazhamalli* that was growing in profusion by the wall. It was still and silent all around. Still. No memory. The *puzha* never remembers. It carries no camera. No suitcase.

I brought out my *veena* and sat down on my stage in the back porch. Lucky yawned loudly and lay down behind me, pushing his paws into the small of my back and stretching. He was fast asleep before the first strains of the *veena* had died away.

That night, as I played, I felt myself melting away. There was no me. There was only the sound of music as it drew from the five elements and created a sixth one. The reverberations grew until each note hung pure and true in the air, like a bubble. Like a droplet of rain quivering at the tip of a new leaf just before dissolving…merging with the moonbeams…with the *puzha*…with the rustle of the *peepul* leaves.

In that instant, I crossed over to the other side. I was looking down into the valley of clouds. When I opened my eyes, there was silence. The same silence as before except that the sound from the valley still lingered in my head.

I looked about me. I had just given the greatest performance of my life and there had been nobody to listen, except the *puzha* and the *devi*. And they didn't know how to say the things that I, an ordinary mortal that I am, wanted to hear. I had no illusions about my capabilities. I knew that that moment might never come again. A coconut shell cannot contain the ocean.

~

*B*ut I was wrong. There had been somebody to listen. Solomon. I saw him only when I was getting up to go back inside. He was leaning against one of the pillars and crying as if his heart was breaking. Silent tears. Tears of torment, the reason for which he would not tell a soul. And I could not guess. If I had, perhaps… . But what's the use? Hindsight! Why do we have so much of the *hind* and hardly any of the *fore*?

I left him there in the porch. I felt he wanted to be alone. It was a feeling I was experiencing more and more often. There was no place for anybody else in the tormented world he was living in those days. I went back into the house and sat down, feeling sad. My heart felt as if its sinuses were blocked. What had happened to Solomon? Why was he so desperately unhappy? I didn't want him to be like that. I wanted him to be the way he was in my early days at Kunnathur. That Solomon had been wise, caring and strong. This Solomon was crumbling inside. Defeated. It made me feel scared and unsure.

Twenty Four

*F*rom our little office on the ground floor at Alanghat, on one hot and still summer afternoon, I could hear the sound of carts as they groaned along on the road to Cheriathur on the other side of the *puzha,* their bells ringing merrily away, in tune with the swing of the bullocks. It sounded like a long line of carts. Each cart picked up the refrain from the one in front as they rattled and rolled into Cheriathur. *The wheels of the cart go round and round. Round and round... .*

The sound made me drowsy but I couldn't afford the luxury of taking a nap that afternoon Solomon, Shailaja and I were preparing a sort of report on the centre's activities in its first year. We were planning to invite the people of Kunnathur to Alanghat, to show them what we had been doing and what our plans for the future were. That way, Solomon said, maybe we would be able to include more people in our work and win their support. We had reached the part in the report that dwelled on our plans to create a Trust and to call the centre, *Sakhi*. We had listed the names of the Trustees — Solomon, Nandu, Shailaja, me and Krishnankutty. It stopped there.

Aaftab's name would have been put down too, if he had kept in touch with us, but he hadn't. There had been no news from him at all. Maybe I had imagined the whole thing. Imagined that there had been some magic between us. Imagined that he cared. Read too much into his manner. After all, he hadn't actually said anything. I stared out of the window, slowly aware of the sound of the bells. I turned back to Solomon. He was thinking too. We were all supposed to be thinking of two more people who could be made Trustees. My mind had wandered off, as usual. In any case, I couldn't think of anybody. Saramma was dead and Aaftab had disappeared. The only other person I could think of was Muthote Shankaran Nayar.

Then suddenly the names came to me in a sort of flash. Just as the other two looked up and were about to say something I quickly opened my mouth, to get there first. And we all said it together. My parents!

~

*M*y relationship with my mother had taken a turn for the better. It had evolved from the turbulence of a mountain stream into the

248

placidity of a benign river flowing in the peaceful countryside. We were still the same people. I don't think we had changed in any way. It's just that we tacitly agreed to accept each other the way we were. We gave each other a wide berth, chose our words carefully and kept short memories. And slowly, with each letter, with each phone call, with each amicable silence in-between, our relationship finally had some air to breathe, like an asthmatic who had been caught in a spasm for thirty years.

I felt good making them the Trustees of my centre — of *Sakhi*. It gave me a sense of togetherness. Of family.

~

*T*he next day I went around to all the houses in Kunnathur — there were about forty-five of them — and began inviting all the villagers to the meeting. I had thought it would be a fairly easy job, something that wouldn't take more than an hour and a half. Step in. Invite. Step out. Next house.

That just shows how distanced, how estranged I was from the villagers. It didn't take me an hour and a half, it took me four days to finish all the houses. And none of the villagers allowed me to leave without drinking something or eating something or both. They made me sit down, they switched on the fan, they brought out all the food they had and stood around beaming, while I ate. Then they walked up with me to the next house, to return home only when the people there had taken over. This happened in every house, including V.K. Menon's.

I hadn't seen him after the time I had waved a crowbar at him in Shankaran Nayar's house. Unsure of how to handle him, I had left him for last. I entered warily, mentally prepared to be insulted and thrown out. The front door was open. Nobody closes doors in Kunnathur. I knocked on the panel and V.K. Menon came out to see who it was. I stood staring at him, feeling terribly uncomfortable. I wondered if I should apologize for waving the crowbar at him. He in turn, looked at me first in shock and then uneasily, pulling his *banian* down tight, in a nervous action.

After an awkward pause, he spoke in a slightly embarrassed manner, thanking me for coming over despite the way he had behaved. The minute he said that, I interrupted him and apologized for behaving the way I did. We went on in that vein for quite some time, interrupting each other's apologies with fresh ones. Then we praised each other to the skies. When we ran out of apologies and praises, a deafening silence filled the room. I stared down at the red oxide floor, listening to the steady squeak of the ceiling fan, trying to fit it into *Vilamba aadi taal*. Tired of doing that, I sat back in my chair and crossed my legs, knitting my fingers together around my knees and stared at the walls. There was an Ajanta clock on one wall, surrounded by four calendars. One of them had a colourful picture of Hanuman wearing pink silk, ripping his chest open and showing the photograph of Rama, Lakshmana and Sita — complete with bows, arrows and crowns — that he carried in his heart. The calendars had withered flowers stuck into their spines.

I turned to look at V.K. Menon. He was looking at his hands, clasped in his lap. I knew enough of Kunnathur society to know that it wasn't time for me to leave yet. I could hear hectic activity in the kitchen and I saw V.K. Menon's daughter come out into the middle room with a kitchen towel flung over her shoulder. We smiled at each other and she again disappeared into the kitchen. I was going to have to eat again.

I returned to *Vilamba aadi taal*, tightening and releasing my abdomen to the rhythm of the fan, when V.K.Menon cleared his throat. I looked up expectantly. He hadn't finished apologizing. He said he hadn't known about Lucky and the way my Trax had been shattered. He said that Shankaran Nayar had told him that he had visited me and offered to help in whatever way he could, in his capacity as Panchaayat President. According to Shankaran Nayar, I had insulted him, using very vulgar language and had made fun of him in front of Devi. That was why V.K. Menon had behaved the way he did. It was only after reading the article in the paper, after I had been jailed, that he realized he hadn't been told the truth.

I stared at him in silence, not knowing what to say — a feeling of acute distaste filling me. I was really fed up of that whole episode and I didn't feel like vindicating myself all over again. At the same time, I knew that some reply was expected of me. In the end I told him that I had no political aspirations and that Shankaran Nayar's fears in that regard were quite unfounded. All the work I was doing was out of a personal interest. Using this as a cue, I told him about the meeting I was planning and invited him to come to Alanghat so that I could explain to him the nature of our work. I said I realised that what I was doing had never before been done in Kunnathur and would take some time to be properly understood. He nodded his head in agreement when I said that and we lapsed into silence again.

This time the silence lasted till his wife came out and invited me into the middle room. There was a small wash basin in one corner and I washed my hands there before seating myself at the formica-topped table. As usual, I was the only one eating while the others stood around and watched. After I had eaten as much as I could, the daughter brought out her two-month-old son and I crooned over him for some time. I was feeling sick and was longing to get back home and eat some Digene.

Finally, when the appropriate length of time had passed, I thanked them and as I turned to leave, V.K. Menon coughed and said, 'Nammale theti therikyerde' – don't misunderstand us. Then he said in English, 'We are all mosque-weetos at the feet of the Lord.' He gazed at me with is hands folded, his eyes earnest and serious. I smiled, shook my head and climbed into the Trax. How can you stay angry with a person who with all seriousness calls himself a "mosque-weeto"?

I drove off with a pillow-case full of mangoes resting in the back seat, it's ripe aroma pervading the Trax and symbolizing peace between V.K. Menon and me. Shankaran Nayar was another matter altogether.

~

*T*hat night Aaftab called. I still remember how grateful I felt for that one act of his. It erased all the pain in one magnificent sweep. That's all it took — one phone call. It was devoid of apologies or even an explanation for the month-long silence but it was enough to make little bubbles of happiness burst in my heart and for my eyes to sing again. Not that we discussed anything earth shattering. He didn't ask me to marry him, if that's what you're wondering. We talked about airfares, I remember. I also remember that he had some problem with his life insurance. Whatever it was, it was way past midnight before I hung up and floated back into my room.

For the first time in more than a month, I allowed myself the luxury of thinking about that Guruvayur trip we took together. I haven't told you the whole story, you know. We didn't drive straight back home as I said we did. We drove up to a rubber estate that belonged to some friends of Aaftab. The Trax broke down on the way back from the estate, not on the way out of Guruvayoor. The owners of the estate lived in Trivandrum, having left the estate in the hands of an estate-manager. So we had the whole place to ourselves and what a wonderful time we had! The estate was high up in the hills, with a stream flowing through it. We went for long walks and we paddled about in the river, trying to catch fish. It felt so good to laugh again and to feel beautiful. I felt like a coconut tree enjoying the first rain of the season. Have you seen a coconut tree in the rain? It does this wild dance, shaking all it's fronds and rocking on its base, trying to wash off the memory of the long, blazing summer.

That coffee estate is the only place in this world that I know of where you can ask for a rainbow and actually get it. We played badminton on our first afternoon there. The sun was shining and everything was bright and cheerful. Suddenly it started raining — one of those freak showers I suppose. It stopped as suddenly as it had started only seconds later. Aaftab and I stood there laughing, looking around and above wondering where the rain had gone. He turned to me and said 'Don't you think this calls for a rainbow?' And *lo and behold*, the most magnificent rainbow I had ever seen emerged right before our eyes, framing the blue-green hills and smiling down on us, making the little champagne bubbles of happiness burst in my heart.

We didn't sleep those two nights. We made love. We counted moles, tasted each others skin and thought of a hundred different ways to make the night last forever. There was a music system in the bedroom and Aaftab had brought some cassettes with him. We listened to music that night with our bodies together — to McCoy Tyner, Dizzy Gillespie, Max Roach and Louis Armstrong. At dawn, for a change of scene, we listened to Bade Ghulam Ali Khan *Sahab* and Begum Akhtar. That was the first night. The second night, we forgot to switch on the music system. By the time we remembered, it was no longer necessary.

~

As we drove down the winding roads of the estate, on our way back to Kunnathur, I heard the call of a wild peacock. It was the most desolate, plaintive and beautiful sound I have ever heard. The peacock spoke my language and spoke of the things I wanted to say. A second later, in the silent distance, I heard an answering call. Somehow, that second call seemed to me to be very significant. A peg to hang my hopes on.

However, to be on the safe side, I locked those two days away in a secret chamber, deep in my heart. I had learnt the art of self preservation.

Twenty Five

Thiruvathira Njaatuvela

*T*hat year the rains were right on schedule. We had had our first monsoon downpour in late May, the month of *Edavam*. On the twenty second of June, the first day of *Thiruvathira Njaatuvela*, it would be two years since I sat waiting for Nandu on that railway platform in Cheriathur. Two whole years. And one lifetime.

~

*T*he sky had been clear and blue when I woke up one morning, in early June. But as the day progressed, it grew sullen and overcast. Dark clouds filled the sky, casting a shadow over Alanghat. At the first hint of actual rain in the air — I don't know how we know, we just seem to sense it — I left the kitchen and walked out into the back yard. The clouds were hanging low beyond the railway bridge and the mild wind was ruffling the leaves of the trees. The wind wasn't actually mild; it was looking for a chance to turn into a gale but something was holding it back on a leash. The air was warm and heavy. I walked out to the tamarind tree growing near the tank house. Under it, a brown and white dog with droopy ears lay nursing eight puppies. Lucky's wife and children. A few months ago this droopy-eared thing had turned up at our doorstep, bag and baggage. Her luggage consisted of a long tail which she continued to wag even while sitting on it, a pink tongue which was perpetually hanging out and two long droopy ears like a schoolgirl's pony tails. She said Lucky drove her wild. It was either Lucky or spinsterhood for her. So we got them married. And in due course, as the *Amar Chitra Katha*s say, Ammini gave birth to eight puppies.

I picked up the sack on which they were lying, trying to dodge Ammini's tongue, and put them in a big basket. As I was carrying the basket into the house, I saw the gate of the *padipera* open and a lady walk in. Leaving the basket in the warm kitchen, I walked around to the front porch. Only when we were almost face-to-face did I recognise her. She was V.K.Menon's wife, Janaki.

~

*W*e sat down and talked about the rains — always a hot topic for discussion in Kunnathur. Then, just as the first drops of rain splattered on the bottom step of the porch, she said something, the shock of which nearly killed me. She said that she was Shankaran

Nayar's sister. Just like that. Out of the blue. With no "reference to context". Hadn't she ever been to school? Didn't she know about an introduction, a body and a conclusion? I stared at her dumbfounded. She looked back at me through the thick lense of her glasses and proceeded to dumbfound me even further — an impossible task but one that she accomplished without any difficulty at all. She said that she had gone to Shankaran Nayar and told him that she planned to join me in my work and help in any way she could, and that there was nothing he could do to stop her. She said that he was one man who had brought nothing but misery and unhappiness to everybody around him, including his children. She lapsed into silence, breathing fast, her spectacles spilling over most of her face.

I was still in shock, sitting there with my mouth open. I blabbered something about not having any intentions of standing for *panchaayat* elections, so he had no cause for worry. She looked up at that and stared at me, long and hard. 'You should,' she said. 'The whole of Cheriathur and Kunnathur want you to, don't you know that? There is not a single man or woman in this area who will not support you. It's time you knew that. That is why Shankaran Nayar is scared.'

We sat in silence for some time. The porch had become dark because of the rain that was now pelting down good and hard. In that brief silence, all that could be heard was the sound of that rain. It sounded like fish frying on a high flame. I sat there listening in surprise to what that lady was telling me. I lifted my head to look at her and she continued, 'You've locked yourself up in this huge house. You don't visit anybody and you don't talk to anybody. You're like a cat with her eyes closed. You've got your eyes closed but we can see you very clearly! All of us are not Shankaran Nayars, you know. Did you know that first time you were interviewed by those big newspaper people it was the only thing we could talk about for days? But how will you know? You want to shut us all out and pretend that Alanghat is Kunnathur. It is not and it is time you realised that.'

By this time I was feeling properly rebuked. I felt as if I were back in school and being scolded for not trying harder. *You have the capacity but you are far too lazy to make the effort. I have a good mind to retain you in the same class for another year.* Suddenly Janaki started laughing. She leaned forward in her chair and patted my hand. 'I am a retired school principal. Sometimes I forget that I have retired. Don't worry — you'll get used to it.'

Janaki Teacher left as soon as the rain subsided, but not before telling me more about Shankaran Nayar's diabolical activities. Apparently, his eldest daughter had committed suicide many years ago. At that time, Shankaran Nayar was living in Calcutta and Janaki Teacher had been in Trivandrum where both she and V.K. Menon were working. Shankaran Nayar had got his daughter married at the age of sixteen, to a "tenth-standard-fail, good-for-nothing" man just so that he had someone to look after his property here, in Cheriathur. Nobody could understand why he did that. There was no earthly reason to pick someone off the street and get his daughter married to him. The child was still studying and doing reasonably well at school. Shankaran Nayar himself was by no means poor and illiterate, or bound by financial worries. So why?

Nobody had an answer to that *why*. That was just Shankaran Nayar being himself. The whole of Cheriathur and Kunnathur watched as that man, Shankaran Nayar's son-in-law, stripped his wife off all her jewelry, then all her expensive saris and finally, off all her dignity. He kept another woman right under her nose, in her own house, while treating her like a servant. He also gave her four children, with barely a year's gap between each. When she couldn't stand it anymore, she wrote to her parents and asked them to take her back. Shankaran Nayar wrote back saying that she would have to retrieve all the gold and money before she could return to his house. He had been, even then, a contemptuous, vicious man who had never forgiven his eldest child for being born a girl. (That's the odd thing about Nayars. Despite being matrilineal and all that, they still want sons. The "family jewels" are very important.) So the poor girl, believing that there was no way out of the hell she was in, drank two bottles of insecticide and died.

She died the night before her mother reached Cheriathur, having left Calcutta without her husband's knowledge, frantic with worry about her daughter. But she was too late, having dithered too long. By the time she reached that purple coloured house, her twenty-two-year-old daughter was already dead, lying on the kitchen floor dressed in a tattered cotton sari, with cockroaches crawling all over her.

Shankaran Nayar returned to Cheriathur soon after that tragedy and refused to have anything to do with his daughter's children — or as he put it, "the children of that murderer" — conveniently forgetting that they were also his grandchildren and that he was as much to blame for that poor child's death as his son-in-law. So the children were taken away by the father and as far as Shankaran Nayar was concerned, the whole chapter was closed.

This was the man I had chosen for an enemy.

~

I don't really know why she did that, but Janaki returned home and phoned her brother, telling him that I had expressed a desire to stand for those wretched *panchaayat* elections. I can only believe that she did it out of hatred for her brother and not out of any desire to make matters worse between him and me. In every other way, Janaki has been behind me like a rock. It is because of her that our Journal Club took off the way it did and it is also because of her that we were able to start our mobile libraries and the scholarship program for girls.

Nevertheless, if I could turn back the clock and was given the power to change just one event — just *one* is enough — I would make her take back that one line about me standing for elections.

That single line paved the way for a devastating loss, so painful that for a while I feared that time will never heal it.

Twenty Six

*F*rom then on, the nightmare never ceased. I was caught in a cyclone — a cyclone so merciless that it left me for dead without a backward glance. Some days after Janaki's visit, Nandu brought me a copy of a local newspaper, published from Cheriathur. It was one of those sleazy three-page things with a smudged print on cheap paper. Nandu sold this paper in his shop, along with more respectable dailies.

I had hit the headlines again. But this time, it was not just me alone. Solomon featured too. The paper alleged that I was using Alanghat as a brothel and that Solomon was a pimp. It said that the centre was only a foil and that, the truth was that I was luring poor village women with the promise of money and making them act in illegal blue films that were filmed by Solomon. It went on about how I had made crores selling these films to rich sheiks in

Dubai and how I planned to move out of Kunnathur as soon as I had made enough to live like a queen for the rest of my life. In the last paragraph it said that Solomon and I were really lovers and were very happy that Saramma had so obligingly died. It claimed that Solomon had moved in with me only a few days after the death of his wife and that we were now living together.

I felt as if someone had slapped me hard. I stood there holding that miserable rag, staring at Nandu. We stood like that for what seemed like a long time till Nandu said, in such a low tone that I had to strain my ears to catch his words, 'Solomon hasn't seen this yet. Shall I buy up all the papers and burn them?' I nodded, pushing my hair back, trying to think. We got into the Trax just as it began to rain. We turned into the main road and there, on every wall, was a caricature of me in the nude. Underneath were some words scrawled in Malayalam. I drove about staring around me, unable to believe that something so horrible could actually be happening to me. I turned to a corner and saw Solomon. He was standing in the rain without a shirt on. His shirt was crumpled into a ball in his hand and with it he was trying to erase one of those grotesque caricature of me. His hand moved in a tired, hopeless sort of way and his head was hanging low as if he couldn't bear to look up.

Poor Solomon. My best friend, my father and my mother, my teacher, my everything. He had given to me the most precious gift of all — a reason to live. And now here he was, standing bare-bodied in the rain, wiping away the stain on my honor with his shirt, the expression on his face defying all description.

The people of Kunnathur reacted to this whole episode in a funny manner. None of them washed their walls or had them repainted. They just pretended the caricatures weren't there. They all turned up in full force that weekend, for the meeting I had invited them for only a few days ago. What do I tell you about that meeting? Well, by mid-morning everybody was there, sitting in Alanghat's wide porch. Devi served some coffee and *vadas,* I think. She did it on her own, without waiting for any instructions from me. By then, I had sort of lost interest in everything. I just sat in the rear verandah with Lucky, watching the *puzha.* She had filled out again, looking strong and capable. Perhaps she knew and was prepared for something that I knew nothing about.

The humiliation had been too much for me to continue pretending that it was all okay. The sight of Solomon, looking so frail and defeated, standing in the rain trying to erase that horrendous thing on the wall never left me, even for a moment. It was always there, being played again and again as if by automatic-replay on a screen somewhere in my mind. Why *Solomon?* Why pick on him? What had he ever done to anybody to deserve this?

Deep down, beyond all the questions and indignation and humiliation, I was scared. Solomon had begun to frighten me. I was no longer sad or worried; now it was fear. Something was gnawing away at his insides — something malignant and I could not help him with it. In our relationship, the help was all one-way — from him to me. Now that it was time for me to do something,

I found myself a miserable failure. I didn't know what to do. I could only stand around and watch. Perhaps some of you know the feeling. But for those of you who don't, my only prayer is that you never have to experience it. I would have done anything for Solomon and that is the irony of the whole thing. I would readily have done anything, and I was made to do the hardest thing of all. I was made to stand around and watch.

~

Vidhi, they call it. Destiny, is it? I don't know. I don't know anything anymore. You decide.

~

When the porch was full of people and it looked as if most of them had arrived, Shailaja came to call me. She had somehow taken on the responsibility of keeping the show going, talking to all the visitors and handing our report around and things like that.

We walked out together. I took one look at all the people there and nearly fainted with fright. The entire place was packed with people! All of Kunnathur was there. Binkity was there, the shopkeepers from Trichur who sold our oil were there too, and so was the journalist from the newspaper. Then there were people I didn't even recognize. I hadn't called all these people. Where had they come from? How had they known? And what was I going to say to all of them? I turned abruptly and went back inside, unable to face the crowd.

Lying in bed, watching the fan rotate above, I could hear Shailaja's voice as she took charge of the meeting. I listened to her as she began the story of the centre; the way we began, how it grew, the problems we faced.… . Binkity asked several questions. I could recognize that *Horn Please OK* voice anywhere! But I knew the questions were asked not so much because he was critical but because he wanted to help in getting the message across. Slowly, Shailaja grew more confident and her voice lost that bleat-like quality it had when she began talking. It made me smile a little bit.

I turned my attention back to the meeting, and realized that she had stopped talking. There was now an uncanny silence. I lay there waiting for some sound. But there wasn't any. I got up slowly and walked back to the front door and peeped out of the window that opened into the porch. Solomon was walking slowly up the drive. Every pair of eyes in the porch was fixed on him but he continued to walk, never once looking up, never once acknowledging anybody. He reached the porch and walked to Shailaja and made her sit down. He stood there for a second, his face turned away, steeling himself. Then, with a long, quivering breath, he turned around and faced the people. My heart plummeted to my feet. Solomon was going to speak. I instinctively knew that nothing would ever be the same again. The lingering hope that that all this would pass and we would return to our old happy selves, died. I clutched the bars of the window with both hands, my forehead resting on them, and waited.

~

*H*is voice sounded clear that morning. Not dry and paper-like, as it usually did. It reminded me of something I couldn't quite put my finger on.

'My name is Solomon,' he said. 'I live in Manuthy and my wife, Saramma recently died of cancer. He paused, took a deep breath and continued. 'My relationship with this child—' he indicated where I was standing and I felt a ripple run down my spine; he had seen me standing there, '—is a complicated one. It is the one beautiful bond that I have been able to forge in this otherwise wretched life of mine. I beg of you not to malign it. His voice broke at this and he remained silent for a long time. Then he looked up, over the heads of the people, over the treetops, to a place in the horizon. He stood like that for a long time but nobody moved, nobody fidgeted. They all waited. He slowly returned and continued, his voice taking on that haunting clarity again. Suddenly I realised what it reminded me of. It reminded me of that wild peacock in the hills of that rubber estate. It had the same wistful quality; it was the same song.

'I have a story to tell you. A story that I have tried to forget for forty years but have failed miserably. Now I have stopped trying. It is my shadow and I can't amputate it.' Another pause. 'I was born here, in this house — in Alanghat — and I lived here for twenty years. My name in those days was Narayanankutty.' His voice was raw and bleeding when he said, 'I am this child's *Ammaman*, her uncle, her mother Ammu's elder brother.' He lifted his hand towards me as he said this and turned to look at me. We stared at each other for a long moment, his eyes clear and piercing and mine befuddled, dazed, stunned. His next lines were intended solely for me.

'I killed a man. Not just any man. I killed the man who meant the whole world to me. I loved the man that I killed. Can you understand that? I wanted to kill him but I didn't want him to die. But he did die. Right here, in front of me. At my feet. And I didn't die with him. I lived...for forty years. For forty years now, I have lived with that memory.

For years my life was a sandstorm. The sand of my thoughts hit my eyes constantly. It covered me from head to toe — my mouth, my throat...everywhere, sand and nothing but sand. After my release, I worked for a few years as an accountant in Madras. That is when I converted to Christianity and changed my name to Solomon. I didn't want anybody — *anybody* to know that I was the miserable wretch who had killed his uncle. I didn't want to see anybody and more importantly, I didn't want anybody to see me. I wanted to bury myself in my shame.

Soon after that, I left for Dubai. By that time, my mother had already disappeared. It is my deepest fear that she had been driven insane by grief for me. In Dubai, I worked and I worked — trying not to think about my uncle or my grandfather or my mother. I put everything I had into my work. My only connection with Kunnathur was through Parameshwaran. I couldn't shake him loose, much as I tried.' Solomon stopped here to smile. It was not a happy smile. Tears ran silently down his wrinkled cheeks, as if without his permission. 'Parameshwaran... he and I had studied together. He would come to the jail to visit me, even though I would refuse to see him every single time. I refused to meet everybody, even my mother. He would also write to me regularly, but never get a reply — hardly ever. But he wrote nevertheless, for old times' sake. He kept in touch with my sister too and that is how I knew that she had a daughter. *You.*

Then, in his last letter to me, the letter he wrote just before he died, he said that he had spent all his life — from the age of six onwards — following me about. And now...now he was tired...tired, old and sick. He said he was handing in his resignation. He died before he could read my reply.'

Solomon stopped here. His mouth was dry and he was talking with difficulty. He reached out for a glass of water from a tray kept on the sill and drank it in unsteady gulps, his hand trembling as he held the glass. I was trembling too. We stared at each other, oblivious of all the people around us. The whole porch and a wall separated us but in my mind there was no distance between us. Our eyes met and held each other's with much intensity across that space.

'By then, I had married Saramma. She was a nurse in Dubai. With her, I entered a relatively more peaceful phase of my life. I read a lot, I worked hard and most of the time, I was able to come to terms with my past. *Most* of the time...' His words were rushing now, as if he wanted to get it over with fast and revert to his usual silence. 'When we retired, we returned to Kerala and settled down in Manuthy. Life was peaceful. Nandu and Shailaja visited us and we enjoyed being with them...we went to church...we lived our lives.

And then you came. A living, breathing image of my uncle. The same laughter, the same eyes, the same hot temper. The same passion for your *veena*. Yet, you were so young and vulnerable. So unhappy. I believed you had been sent to me and that I had to take care of you. The instant I saw you with you head down, on the wheel of your Trax, I knew you needed help and I knew that I was the one who could give it you. I felt as if I had known you forever. I knew your every mood. I could read your thoughts. I knew what you were going to say even before you said it.

You became more than just my niece — my sister's daughter. You were my own child — you were me! Yet... yet, you were a constant reminder of my uncle.' My heart contracted at the way he said that. His voice dipped and he took a long, audible breath. 'I love you. You are the one beautiful thing in my life. I love you and I am so proud of you...so proud!

But at the same time, memories keep returning to haunt me...all those horrible memories...and I relive my guilt everyday...over and over again. I am guilty...guilty of murder. *Kunje* - my child - in my own court, I stand forever guilty.'

~

*H*is eyes were burning against the white of his face and his words hung in the air, refusing to fade away, scorching my heart until it shrieked for mercy. He tore his eyes away from mine and looked at the people sitting in the porch. 'I am telling you all this because I can't bear to see this child humiliated in the way she has been. For me, she is as pure as her name — Anagha, the one without blemish. Please don't allow her to be paraded in the streets like this. I am begging you.' His voice trailed off into mere whisper as he pleaded, '*Madi...Madi*!' Enough...Enough!

He turned around abruptly and walked with leaden feet, out of the porch and down the driveway, his thin, lonely figure whipped by the wind. I stood rooted to the window, staring after him, wanting to call out to him. But I just stood there, clinging to the bars of the window, my head whirling and my heart dying inside me. And so the moment passed.

Twenty Seven

I sat down on a chair nearby. My thoughts felt as if they were stuck, like the spool of a cassette caught in the head of the player. I sat upright, my back rigid, and stared at the red floor at my feet. People were moving about all over the place. I don't know what they were doing. Voices floated back to me. Disjointed. Gibberish. Perhaps they were talking to me but I couldn't make sense of it. I had reached the end of my tether.

It took me more than an hour to unravel the spool and wind it back into the cassette. I knew then that I had to go to Manuthy, to Solomon. I got up, my back aching with the strain of having sat rigidly for so long. My movements were like that of an underwater animal, slow and weightless. I realised it was raining only after I walked out of the house and got drenched instantly. I had to wait almost an hour and a half for the rain to subside.

I drove feeling disoriented and confused. A thousand images flitted across my mind. The memory of Solomon - Narayanankutty - as I showed him around Alanghat. The memory of him telling me the story of Alanghat — of how he had killed his uncle. The memory of his ravaged face the day I yelled at all of them for not telling me that Nandu was in touch with Narayanankutty. My thoughts veered off at a tangent for a split second — Nandu and Shailaja had known all along! Suddenly that became insignificant. How did it matter?

So many signs — that full-moon night when I found him crying after he had heard me play the *veena* -- so many signs and I still hadn't guessed that Solomon was Narayanankutty, the man I had wondered about nearly every day. He had been right next to me all this while. Can you comprehend that? Does it make sense to you? Maybe it does. Maybe it's just I who am the fool.

~

I reached Manuthy by four in the evening. I had to drive slowly because of the rain. The front door was open and I walked in. There was nobody in the small drawing room. I sat down and waited for about five minutes, wondering what I would say to him, feeling nervous — my usually keen instinct failing me completely when I needed it the most; giving me no warning of the ordeal that awaited me. After a while, I got up and went out into the verandah to see if Solomon was out in the garden. But it was raining quite heavily now and so there was no way he could be out there. I went back inside and towards the door of his study. It was closed. I opened it — and there he was. Hanging from the fan.

I looked up at his face and shook his feet but nothing happened. I stopped — maybe I was hurting him! I tried to pull the writing table towards him, knocking everything about as I did so, but it was too heavy. I stood there uncertainly for a second, my heart thumping in my chest and my knees shaking uncontrollably. I had to leave the room and do something but how could I leave him alone? Suppose something happened to him!

Yelling to him that I'll be back in a second, I turned and ran out to the back of the house to fetch a big stool that I knew was kept there. I stumbled and blundered back to the study, the heavy stool obstructing my sight. I could barely carry it but I had to. It seemed imperative to me that I get the stool into that room and do something! I just kept yelling at Solomon to not die. I put the stool next to him and climbed up. As I stood there, my arm around his limp, heavy body — he was so thin, how could he be so heavy — trying to do I don't know what, I realized that it was over. It was no use. I would have to call the police.

~

*T*he police came and cut the rope that held him to the fan. He landed with a thump and I winced, rushing to him to see if he was hurt. But they wouldn't let me near him. I hovered around anyway,

275

in case he wanted something, in case he needed me. The senior policeman walked up to me and said something about a body. He said they were taking the body for a post-mortem and that they would return it to me tomorrow. *Body*? *It*? What was this man talking about? Then he asked me whether I was his — indicating Solomon — next of kin. And I said yes, I was his niece. I stared down at Solomon, lying straight and motionless on the cold hard floor. Slowly it seeped in. Solomon's body. They were taking *it* for a post-mortem. Solomon was dead. He had killed himself.

They carried Solomon into the ambulance and as the doors slammed, I felt a wave of panic rise within me. Where were they taking him? Would he be alright on his own? Maybe I should go with him. I turned to the policeman. 'Will he be okay alone?' He stared back at me impassively, his face expressionless. Then he said softly that Solomon would be fine and that he would be well taken care of. He took me by the elbow and led me to the Trax.

I stared straight in front of me as he drove me home. My thoughts were jumbled. Post-mortem — Solomon would return after his post-mortem. What did they do in a post-mortem? Solomon would know the answer to that. Oh, but I can't ask Solomon. Solomon was dead. He had killed himself. Perhaps he wasn't dead! Perhaps they would find that out during the post-mortem.

~

I found myself in my room at Alanghat, lying in my bed. Lucky was sitting next to me and staring into my face, his nose inches away from mine. I wondered how I had reached there. I turned and saw Krishnankutty sitting by the side of my bed, preparing an injection. He looked at me, stroked my hair and then jabbed my arm.

Twenty Eight

Solomon returned from the post-mortem in a coffin. The funeral was the next day, at the Pentecost Church in Manuthy. A lot of people attended the service and the small church was full, packed to its capacity. That's what they say for cricket matches. *The stadium was packed to its capacity.* Well, the church was packed to its capacity that day — the day of Solomon's funeral. He was dead — killed himself.

I stared out of the window trying to block out the words of the priest. He was lying. I moved restlessly in my seat and Shailaja, sitting next to me, reached out to touch me. I moved away. Everybody was lying to me. The fact was that I was alone again. I had nobody. From now on there was just me and the world. Nobody to fall back on. Nobody to dodge behind. Nobody to run to. There was just me. Solo.

I tried to remember all the things he had told me. Something about remembering and forgetting and memory and stuff. What was the use of all that now? Was it of any use? It couldn't stop the pain. It couldn't bring Solomon back. It couldn't rewrite my family's history. It couldn't give me another face, a face that didn't resemble Raman Nayar's. It couldn't do anything. Not one bloody thing. Those were just was a whole lot of nice sounding words. Theory. *The Principles and Practices of Life and Living.* Good for a B.A. degree but that's about it. Not one single useful tip on how to cope with death. *Solomon's* death. A mad urge rose in me to walk up to the coffin, open one of his eyes and tell him that it wasn't working. But he was dead — had been dead for two days. I had to keep looking at the coffin kept in the aisle to convince myself.

The service over, Nandu and some other people got up to lift the coffin and I followed them out of the church. I had requested the priest to allow me to bury Solomon at Alanghat and he had agreed. It started raining again as we left the church. As I was climbing into the hearse, I saw the journalist from the newspaper standing and watching me from across the road. He was leaning against the door of a small tea-shop and smoking a cigarette. I looked away quickly — he reminded me of Muthote Shankaran Nayar and the *panchaayat* elections. I flashed another look at the journalist. He was still watching me, his face shrouded in swirls of cigarette smoke. Across the road, through the falling rain, our eyes met. We both knew then that I was going to stand for those elections and that I was going to make sure that Shankaran Nayar lost. We both knew and each knew that the other knew. He tossed the cigarette into a puddle and walked away. I got into the hearse and sat by the head of the coffin. It was still open and I could see Solomon's face. It was smooth and suddenly unlined. He seemed to be smiling. I wondered what the joke was.

The hearse drove slowly in the blinding rain all the way back to Kunnathur and as we entered the gates of Alanghat — kept wide open to welcome Narayanankutty — I saw the entire village standing there. Not sheltering themselves under the porch but standing outside, in the rain, next to the little grove of coconut trees that I chosen as Solomon's final resting place. From here, if he ever chose to return, he would be able to see Alanghat, the *puzha*, the *pavizhamalli*, the *peepul* trees, the *kani konda* and the blue skies above.

As they lowered the coffin into his grave, I remembered the first time I saw him and my eyes filled up. The last two years passed like a silent movie through my mind. I had so many memories of Solomon, so many precious memories. I stared down at the coffin, deep in its grave, hot tears running down my rain-wet cheeks. I wanted to jump in and follow him.

The priest was talking again. 'Ashes to ashes, dust to dust... .' I wasn't really listening. I couldn't concentrate. All I knew was that I wasn't ready to let-go. A part of me hated myself for being so small and selfish, and as I heard the drone of the priest's voice, that part grew bigger and bigger until, in one massive wrench, I tore myself away from my own grief.

Kneeling down on the soft, wet earth with folded hands, I fumbled for words. A prayer. My chin wobbled and I was breathing in shuddering gasps. For an instant, I almost gave up. The pain was too much. I closed my eyes and swallowed the huge raw lump that was stuck in my throat and pictured him in the sunlight, his white hair glistening, his white clothes dazzling and blinding me. I pictured him smiling.

And then the prayer came. I prayed for the Solomon's soul. Narayanankutty's soul. I prayed for everlasting peace. No more pain. No torment. Eternal freedom. Tears still rolled down my cheeks as I picked up a fistful of earth and dropped it into Solomon's grave, bidding him farewell.

The grave was filling up fast. When I couldn't see the coffin anymore, I turned and walked to one of the coconut trees and sat down. Lucky appeared from somewhere and we sat there together, cheek-to-cheek. People were now leaving, pressing my shoulder or taking my hands in theirs as they passed. I leaned against the trunk of the tree and closed my eyes.

When I opened them again, I was alone with Lucky. Solomon's grave was covered completely and the freshly dug-up earth was piled in a neat mound. It had started drizzling again. Somewhere at the back of my mind, I remembered it was the twenty second of June, the first day of *Thiruvaathira Njaatuvela*. The time of heavy rain.

I sat under the coconut tree getting drenched as the drizzle turned into a heavy downpour, flattening the mound of earth over Solomon's grave. My thoughts wandered, only to return like iron filings to a magnet, to the fact that Solomon was dead. Ashes to ashes, dust to dust. I thought of my mother. She and my father would be here soon. She would relive the entire nightmare all over again. I thought of my father — married to a woman who dragged her past around with her like a ball and chain. He hadn't been spared either. We had all paid, each one of us. But Solomon had paid more than the rest of us. Had paid dearly.

It was getting late. Almost dark. I turned to look at the house and found myself looking straight at Aaftab. Nandu was standing behind him. He must have phoned him and told him that Solomon was dead. I hadn't been capable of doing anything. My eyes moved back to Aaftab. There was a look of disbelief in those black eyes, mixed with grief and anger. *This is not the way it's supposed to be*! I watched him as he walked up to me. He sat down by my side, with his knees drawn up and his hands hanging loose between them.

Aaftab stared for a long time at Solomon's grave — working things out, fighting a battle with himself, trying to tell Solomon that it was okay and that he understood. When he turned to look at me, it was pitch dark and I couldn't see his face anymore. But I sensed that the anger had gone. His hand groped in the dark and I slipped mine into it. It felt cold and wet. Two cold hands. Two bereft people.

And that's how we sat, Aaftab and I, until dawn; keeping

Solomon company as he embarked on his journey to the realm beyond the ether. Back to Shiva.

Twenty Nine

Karkitakam Sankramam

A cold gray wind blew in from the *puzha* early one morning. Laden with the fragrance of wet earth and memories of a thousand rains gone by, it shook the trees, created ripples in the *puzha* and drove the rain into the porch, almost knocking me off-balance and tossing the jasmine that crept up the pillars to the roof. The creeper had bloomed in the night and had carpeted the ground with its sweet white flowers, as if to receive the wind. The more it whistled and blew, the happier she got, till weary, it receded leaving the rain and *puzha* to follow their own will.

I watched with unseeing eyes as the *puzha* went about her business. It was our weeding day, Aaftab's and mine. We were driving down to the Registrar's office at ten o'clock, with my parents, Nandu and Shailaja and after that I would be Aaftab's wife. My dearest wish was coming true and all I could think of was that Solomon would not be there. My Solomon was dead. Why couldn't I get that out of my head just this once and be happy? Revel in this moment of joy. Take what I was getting. After all, it was what I wanted more than anything else.

For the *puzha* it was business as usual! How could she be so stoic? Didn't she know that Solomon was dead? Of course she knew — she was there when it happened. She was there then, but had flowed on without stopping. My hold-all of grief, my countless plastic bags of memories and my suitcases of self-pity!

I walked out of the porch, into the rain. It was only a few steps from there to Raman Nayar's steps, and so the rain had time only to beat a sort of *chakkardhar* on my head, wet my shoulders and spike my eyelashes, clinging to them in tiny rainbow droplets. The steps were wet despite the tiled protection and the many hued bougainvillea that grew wild over it. I walked down carefully, gripping the railing. The steps were covered green with moss and were dangerously slippery. If I wasn't careful, I'd go the Keshavan Nayar way and that wouldn't be very funny – not on my wedding day. In any case, there was no need for the entire Alanghat family to fall headlong to their death. There were other dramatic deaths to choose from. I could walk out of the house and disappear with the *udianmaar*, I could pretend I was a coconut and have a kitchen knife stuck in my craw – that was a pretty good way, almost as good as falling head-down on a flight of stone steps – or I could…or I could hang myself from a ceiling fan.

I stopped mid-way for a second and was about to carry on

when I heard a sound behind me. I turned around to find Lucky staring at me in a '*Have you gone mad? It's raining!*' sort of way; looking comical with his half-wet fur standing up in spikes and a large drop of water on his nose. I turned back and continued down the steps. Behind me, I could hear him patter clumsily down but he stopped again and barked once. A short one. I knew the meaning of that bark. It meant that I didn't have his support on this particular expedition.

I reached the river and climbed down even further until the water circled round my legs, feeling cold and fresh. I turned to look at Lucky. He was still standing there in suspended animation, half of him on the higher step and the rest of him on the lower one. *Trishanku Swargam.* I went deeper into the water, my nightgown billowing about me like a blue parachute, and sat down on the last step. The waters of the *puzha* swirled around my shoulders and I felt tiny fish nibble at my feet. Lucky barked again, slightly hysterically this time. When I ignored him, he threw caution to the wind and clambered down, his claws failing to get a grip on the moss-covered steps. He skidded down the last step, flew and fell with a loud splash into the *puzha*, letting out a mighty howl as he hit the cold water. Trying not to laugh — he is very sensitive, you know — I helped him onto dry land, two steps above me, but he wasn't happy there. He climbed down again and stood shivering, three feet in the water and the fourth one on my shoulder, his claws digging into my flesh. A picture of abject misery.

'Nobody asked you to follow me,' I said, and felt his claws

digging deeper into my flesh as he whined. I heard fresh activity behind me and turned to find Aaftab standing and staring at us with his hands on his hips. Lucky let go of my shoulder and clambered onto him, complaining loudly and volubly. Aaftab picked him up, still complaining, and climbed the stairs muttering rather unkindly that he was fed-up of funerals and that if I died, he was going to leave me to bloat and rot in the *puzha*. I listened to him until Lucky and his complaints — what a liar — were out of earshot and resumed my solemn contemplation of the *puzha*.

She had moved on, my *puzha*. She lived on, enjoying this monsoon as if it was the first one she had ever seen. Why couldn't I do that? Why did I feel so heavy and burdened? This was the happiest day of my life, for God's sake! Why was I still stuck in the day Solomon had died. I lowered my head till my cheek touched the water, feeling its soft caress. Then I got up slowly, like a hippo getting out of a swamp. Why couldn't I forget just for an instant and be happy? I had only today to revel in the joy of being married. Tomorrow would make today yesterday. Past tense. Why, *why* couldn't I be like the *puzha*?

I couldn't be like the *puzha* because she was only a body of water. I, on the other hand, was not a body of water! I was a human being with feelings. Bodies of water did not have feelings. That was the difference. That is why she had flowed on — no, *it* had flowed on and I was still stuck where I was. I had loved Solomon. She - *it* - hadn't.

~

*T*hat outburst didn't make me feel any better. So I gave up and went up to my room to change before going down to the kitchen. My mother was there, standing by the hearth and making *dosas* for breakfast. I stood by the door and watched her. She was tall and big-built. Probably the most familiar figure in my life. All her movements were familiar. The way she turned the *dosa* on the *tava*, the way she stood waiting for the *dosa* to cook, the way she peered over her glasses so that she see what she was doing.

Yet, a month ago, as I stood waiting for her and my father to arrive at Cheriathur station, I hadn't the foggiest notion as to how she would react. Would she cry? Would she be philosophical? Or would she be prickly and impatient? I just didn't know. I kept looking at her during the drive back to Kunnathur, trying to fathom her thoughts. She seemed aloof and distant, looking out of the window, barely listening to my father and Aaftab as they talked. They mostly talked about Solomon and about all that had happened in the last two years. I didn't say much as I didn't feel like talking. When Aaftab reached the part about Solomon's death and the funeral, my mother looked down in a jerky movement and then turned to look at me, her hands clutching at her handbag, and her sorrow evident on her face. She looked helpless. Tormented. Suddenly I knew what I had to do. I had to stop being just her daughter. She needed support to get her through what she saw as an ordeal and I knew then that I was the one who was going to give it to her.

I looked back at her and wiggled my eyebrows. I know you probably think that I should have reached out and held her hand. But, in my family we do not touch. We would die of embarrassment if we had to hold hands or hug. My little gesture reassured her and she smiled faintly.

We reached Kunnathur and drove into Alanghat. Nandu and Shailaja were there, waiting for us. Alanghat looked peaceful and happy, as I knew she would. Welcoming. No ghosts leapt out at my parents and I could sense their relief. We sat in the porch after dinner, all of us, sipping coffee and talking softly. Devi and Lakshmi were there too, sitting on the steps and watching my mother. She was a real *tamburatti* and things hadn't changed so much that they were no longer in awe of her. Lucky and his wife had curled up in the centre and gone to sleep. I leaned back in my chair and closed my eyes, listening to Nandu as he said something to my father. You might think I am being fanciful, but at that moment I felt that Solomon was sitting there too, listening to all of us, smiling lovingly. I opened my eyes and looked around. He wasn't there. Not physically, anyway.

Early next morning we went to Solomon's grave. My mother had some fresh flowers in her hand. At the grave she stopped, uncertain of what to do. She turned to look at me and I walked up to her to stand by her side. I took one of the hibiscus from her hand and placed it on Solomon's grave and she followed suit with the rest of the flowers. I had the odd feeling that I had just introduced the two of them to each other. My parents spent a lot of time at Solomon's grave that morning, sitting under a coconut tree — thinking, I suppose, of all the years that had passed, all the things that had happened, how unfinished their relationship with Solomon - Nanu - had been. How unsatisfying. Then they bound all those thoughts together and "cast them into the ocean" — to use Solomon's favorite expression — setting Nanu free forever, and in the process freeing themselves.

After that first visit together, my mother would go to Solomon's grave on her own everyday. And she always took something for him. Usually flowers, but once my father and I saw her sneaking *unniappams* out, bundled up in her *pallu*. She had made them that afternoon. Maybe Solomon had liked *unniappams*. Funny I hadn't known that.

~

*S*tanding in the kitchen, watching her make *dosas*, I thought what a good thing it was, in a way, that she had returned to Alanghat. I was sure that now her wounds would heal. Finally, she would be able to get on with her life. My parents visited Aaftab and me many times after that first visit, and each time they came to Alanghat the bonds were strengthened. I don't know how we managed for so long, thinking that we could live without Alanghat. She was as necessary to us as the air that we breathed. We were of

THE RIVER HAS NO CAMERA

Alanghat. We were her children. We belonged here.

~

*B*y the time we returned from Trichur, it was late in the evening and Aaftab and I had been married for nearly eight hours. We sat around the big kitchen table, tired but happy. Devi and Lakshmi were busy cooking dinner and the kitchen felt homely and warm in the firelight. I turned to look at Aaftab. We smiled at each other and I laid my head on his shoulder — it felt so good to be home at last. Outside, the rain pattered comfortably making me feel even more snug and cozy. That's when I realised that like my *puzha*, I too had flowed along. Perhaps not as swiftly or as relentlessly as the *it* but I hadn't stopped altogether, as I thought I had. And that's when I knew that I would be okay and that one day I would be healed.

Slowly, the conversation died out and one by one, the others left the room — Nandu and Shailaja to return home and my parents, Devi and Lakshmi to go to bed. Aaftab and I continued to sit there, holding hands and planning our future, our life together, thinking of how happy we were going to be and how blessed we were.

We sat there a long time, lost in our own little world. Then the back door opened and Lakshmi came in, looking surprised to see us still sitting there. 'Is this all you can think of doing on your wedding night?' she asked Aaftab in Malayalam. I translated and he grinned at her, not bothering to reply. I looked out of the door, beyond Lakshmi and into the darkness. 'How dark the night is!' I said. Lakshmi turned to look too and said '*Aye hey, id raatri ondu ella - idu pulercha aane.*' The night is over — this is daybreak.

A-WES/1542/06/02